## "You're engaged?"

Tommy couldn't help his shock. He felt gutted. She hadn't been engaged the nights they'd spent together and that was only a couple of weeks ago, or had she? *Since when?*

"It just happened," Bella said, clearly avoiding his eyes.

He shook his head, trying to make sense of this. If there'd been someone special in her life, she would have told him the weekend they were together, wouldn't she? He thought they told each other everything. Or at least used to. *Who?*

She cleared her throat before she spoke. He caught the slight tremor in her lips before she said, "Fitz."

He laughed and said, "That's not even funny." Of course she was joking. They'd grown up with Edwin Fitzgerald Mattson the Third. Or the *turd*, as they'd called him. Fitz had been two years older and the most obnoxious kid either of them had ever met.

# STICKING TO HER GUNS

---

**New York Times** Bestselling Author
## B.J. DANIELS

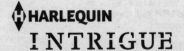

This book is number 115! I dedicate it to all my loyal readers. Thank you so much for making it possible. I always wanted to write stories when I grew up. It took me a while to grow up, LOL, but this is what I love doing. What a joy it is that I can share these stories with you. I hope you enjoy this next Colt Brothers Investigation book. Welcome to Lonesome, Montana.

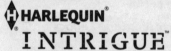

**HARLEQUIN®**
**INTRIGUE™**

PLEASE RECYCLE
THIS PRODUCT IS RECYCLABLE

Recycling programs for this product may not exist in your area.

ISBN-13: 978-1-335-48961-6

Sticking to Her Guns

Harlequin Enterprises ULC
22 Adelaide St. West, 41st Floor
Toronto, Ontario M5H 4E3, Canada
www.Harlequin.com

**Printed in U.S.A.**

**B.J. Daniels** is a *New York Times* and *USA TODAY* bestselling author. She wrote her first book after a career as an award-winning newspaper journalist and author of thirty-seven published short stories. She lives in Montana with her husband, Parker, and three springer spaniels. When not writing, she quilts, boats and plays tennis. Contact her at bjdaniels.com, on Facebook or on Twitter, @bjdanielsauthor.

### Books by B.J. Daniels

### Harlequin Intrigue

#### *A Colt Brothers Investigation*

*Murder Gone Cold*
*Sticking to Her Guns*

#### *Cardwell Ranch: Montana Legacy*

*Steel Resolve*
*Iron Will*
*Ambush Before Sunrise*
*Double Action Deputy*
*Trouble in Big Timber*
*Cold Case at Cardwell Ranch*

#### *Whitehorse, Montana: The Clementine Sisters*

*Hard Rustler*
*Rogue Gunslinger*
*Rugged Defender*

### HQN

#### *Montana Justice*

*Restless Hearts*
*Heartbreaker*
*Heart of Gold*

Visit the Author Profile page at Harlequin.com.

## CAST OF CHARACTERS

*Tommy Colt*—The former rodeo cowboy is ready to tell his best friend, Bella, how he feels about her and that he's staying in Lonesome to join his brother in the PI business. But she has shocking news for him.

*Bella Worthington*—She could see a future with Tommy Colt...until her father's youngest business partner makes her an offer she can't refuse.

*Edwin Fitzgerald Mattson III (Fitz)*—He's always gotten whatever he wanted. Now he wants Bella—any way he can get her.

*Nolan Worthington*—He was the first to admit that he'd made a series of mistakes that now has put not only himself but his daughter in jeopardy.

*James Colt*—The PI is delighted to have his brother join the detective business their father started and didn't get to finish. But now Tommy needs his help to find out why the love of his life is about to marry the wrong man.

*Edwin Fitzgerald Mattson II*—He wishes he could help Bella, but unfortunately he has his own problems.

*Ronan and Milo*—The two thugs were hired to make sure that the wedding goes off without any trouble from Tommy Colt.

*Roberto*—The cook loves making special meals for Bella...even if it means upsetting the man who hired him.

## Chapter One

Bella Worthington took a breath and, opening her eyes, finally faced her reflection in the full-length mirror. The wedding dress fit perfectly—just as he'd said it would. While accentuating her curves, the neckline was modest, the drape flattering. As much as she hated to admit it, Fitz had good taste.

The sapphire-and-diamond necklace he'd given her last night gleamed at her throat, bringing out the blue-green of her eyes—also like he'd said it would. He'd thought of everything—right down to the huge pear-shaped diamond engagement ring on her finger. All of it would be sold off before the ink dried on the marriage license—if she let it go that far.

As she studied her reflection though she realized this was exactly as he'd planned it. She looked the beautiful bride on her wedding day. No one would be the wiser.

She could hear music and the murmur of voices downstairs. He'd invited the whole town of Lonesome, Montana. She'd watched from the upstairs window as the guests had arrived earlier. He'd wanted an audience for this and now he would have one.

The knock at the door startled her, even though she'd been expecting it. "It's time," said a male voice on the other side. One of Fitz's hired bodyguards, Ronan, was waiting. He would be carrying a weapon under his suit. Security, she'd been told, to keep her safe. A lie.

She listened as Ronan unlocked her door and waited outside, his boss not taking any chances. He had made sure there was no possibility of escape short of shackling her to her bed. Fitz was determined that she find no way out of this. It didn't appear that she had.

In a few moments, she would be escorted downstairs to where her maid of honor and bridesmaids were waiting—all hand-chosen by her groom. If they'd questioned why they were down there and she was up here, they hadn't asked. He wasn't the kind of man women questioned. At least not more than once.

For another moment, Bella stared at the stranger in the mirror. She didn't have to wonder how she'd gotten to this point in her life. Unfortunately, she knew too well. She'd just never thought Fitz would go this far. Her mistake. He, however, had no idea how far she was willing to go to make sure the wedding never happened.

Taking a breath, she picked up her bouquet from her favorite local flower shop. The bouquet had been a special order delivered earlier. Her hand barely trembled as she lifted the blossoms to her nose for a moment, taking in the sweet scent of the tiny white roses—also his choice. Carefully, she separated the tiny buds afraid it wouldn't be there.

It took her a few moments to find the long slim silver blade hidden among the roses and stems. The blade was sharp, and lethal if used correctly. She knew exactly how to use it. She slid it back into the bouquet out of sight. He wouldn't think to check it. She hoped. He'd anticipated her every move and attacked with one of his own. Did she really think he wouldn't be ready for anything?

Making sure the door was still closed, she checked her garter. What she'd tucked under it was still there, safe, at least for the moment.

Another knock at the door. Fitz would be getting impatient and no one wanted that. "Everyone's waiting," Ronan said, tension in his tone. If this didn't go as meticulously planned there would be hell to pay from his boss. Something else they all knew.

She stepped to the door and opened it, lifting her chin and straightening her spine. Ronan's eyes swept over her with a lusty gaze, but he stepped back as if not all that sure of her. Clearly he'd been warned to be wary of her. Probably just as she'd been warned what would happen if she refused to come down—or worse, made a scene in front of the guests.

At the bottom of the stairs, the room opened and

she saw Fitz waiting for her with the person he'd hired to officiate.

He was so confident that he'd backed her into a corner with no way out. He'd always underestimated her. Today would be no different. But he didn't know her as well as he thought. He'd held her prisoner, threatened her, forced her into this dress and this ruse.

But that didn't mean she was going to marry him.

She would kill him first.

# *Chapter Two*

*Three weeks earlier*

Bella smiled to herself. She'd just enjoyed the best long weekend of her life. Now sitting in a coffee shop with her closest friend, Whitney Burgess, she blurted out the words she hadn't even let herself voice before this moment.

"I'm in love."

Whitney blinked. They'd just been talking about Bella's new online furnishings business she'd started. "You're in love?" her friend repeated. "With the new line?"

Bella shook her head. "With a man. The man I want to spend the rest of my life with." This was a first so Bella was sure it came as a surprise.

"Love? Marriage?" Whitney laughed. "Seriously? Anyone I know?"

"Maybe. I just spent a long weekend with him in that luxurious hotel downtown. It was amazing."

Her friend shook her head. "And you aren't going to tell me his name?"

"Not yet."

"Well, at least tell me about your weekend," Whitney said, dropping her voice and leaning closer. "Don't leave out a thing."

"We watched old Westerns, made popcorn, ate ice cream, ordered the most wonderful breakfasts in the mornings and had hamburgers and fries at night."

"Wait, you skipped the best part," her friend joked.

"We didn't even kiss." Bella laughed. "It was the most fun I've had on a date in forever."

Whitney sat back. "Sorry, you didn't even *kiss*? So you didn't…for a whole long weekend together?" she asked incredulously.

Bella shook her head. "It was *perfect*."

"Not my idea of the perfect date, but clearly it has you glowing. Come on, who is this amazing man?"

Bella hesitated. "Tommy Colt."

"That wild boy your father ran off the ranch with a shotgun when you two were teenagers?" her friend asked in surprise.

Laughing, Bella nodded. "I think I've been in love with Tommy for years, but I never admitted it, even to myself, until now. We were inseparable from about the time we were five, always sneaking away to see each other. Our ranches are adjacent so it was just a matter of cutting through the woods."

She smiled at the memories. "We built a tree house together at ten. That's about the same time we became blood brothers, so to speak." She held out her finger and touched the tiny scar.

Whitney was shaking her head. "You're really serious?"

"I am. It feels right," she said. "I wanted to wait before I said anything."

"Wait. He doesn't know how you feel about him?"

"Not yet," Bella admitted. "But I think he might suspect. Maybe."

Her friend laughed again. "Why didn't you tell him?"

"I'm waiting for the right time, but I will soon. My dad called. I have to go back to Lonesome. I told Tommy that if he was around…"

Whitney was shaking her head again. "You amaze me. When it comes to business, you don't hesitate. But when it comes to love…"

"I'm cautious."

"No," her friend said. "You're scared. And truthfully, I didn't think anything scared you. Are you worried he doesn't feel the same?"

"Maybe."

"Tell him! He's a rodeo cowboy, right?"

"He's on the circuit right now. I think he has a ride in Texas coming up."

"You could meet him there, surprise him," Whitney suggested, clearly getting into this.

"I could." Bella smiled, the idea appealing to her. "I definitely could." Her smile faded. "But first I have to go to the ranch and see what my father wants." She didn't add that there had been something in his tone that worried her. She just hoped this wasn't another ploy to try to get her to join his business partnership. She didn't trust his other two partners, Edwin Fitzgerald Mattson senior and his son, Fitz.

"I am going to tell Tommy how I feel about him," she said, the decision made. "I'm glad we got together today. I think I'll surprise him in Austin." She just hoped he felt the same way about her.

TOMMY COULDN'T BELIEVE he was home in Lonesome—and for good.

"Okay, Davey and Willie are gone," his brother James said after the others had cleared out. The four brothers had gotten together for the weekend, but now Davey and Willie were headed back to the rodeo circuit, leaving Tommy and James alone.

"Why are you really here, Tommy?"

They were in the upstairs office of Colt Investigations, what would soon be Colt Brothers Investigations, if Tommy had his way.

Before answering, he walked to the second-story window and looked out on the small Western town of Lonesome, Montana. It was surrounded by pines and mountains and a river to the east. He'd grown up here but had been gone for years on the rodeo circuit.

"I told you. I'm done with the rodeo and living my life on the road. I want to join you in our father's private eye business and stick around here."

"What's her name?"

Tommy laughed and turned to smile at his older brother. "So like you to think it has something to do with a woman. Speaking of women, how is Lorelei?" Lori, as they all called her, was his brother's fiancée. They were in the process of having a home built for them on the Colt Ranch.

"Lori's fine. Don't try to change the subject." James leaned back in the old high-backed leather chair behind the marred oak desk. Four years ago it would have been their father sitting there. James looked enough like Del that it still gave Tommy a start. They all had the thick dark hair, the same classic good looks and a dark sense of humor. They all had loved rodeo for as long as they could remember.

Thinking of their father, Tommy felt the loss heart deep. They'd lost their father way too soon. Worse, none of them believed Del's death had been an accident. Tommy had known that coming back here would be painful.

"I want to be part of the business," he said. "I can do this. I know I can."

"You don't know anything about being a private investigator."

"Neither did you," Tommy said. Everything about this room reminded him of their father and the Colt legacy. "But look at you now. A major cold case solved and business picking up."

James shook his head. "I never thought you'd ever quit the rodeo. Not you."

He could feel his brother's gaze on him as he moved around the room. "I used to dream of following in our ancestors' footsteps," Tommy admitted as he studied an old Hollywood poster featuring his great-grandfather Ransom Del Colt. Ransom had been a famous movie star back in the forties and early fifties when Westerns had been so popular.

Their grandfather, RD Colt Jr., had followed in Ransom's footprints for a while before starting his own Wild West show. RD had traveled the world ropin' and ridin'. Tommy and his brothers had grown up on the stories.

He could see himself in their faces as well as his father's and his brothers'. They shared more than looks. They were all most comfortable on the back of a horse—even when it was bucking.

"So what happened?" James asked.

Tommy shook his head. "Recently rodeoing just didn't have that hold on me anymore."

"Uh-huh," his brother said. "You going to tell me about her or not?"

He smiled and continued around the room, looking at all the photographs and posters. The Colts had a rich cowboy history, one to be proud of, his father always told them. And yet their father, Del Colt, had broken the mold. After being a rodeo cowboy, he'd had to quit when he got injured badly.

Del, who'd loved Westerns and mystery movies, had gotten his PI license and opened Colt Investigations, while he'd encouraged them to follow their hearts. He'd taught his sons to ride a horse before they could walk. Their hearts had led them straight to the rodeo—just as it had Del and the Colt men before them.

Tommy had thought that he would never stop living and breathing rodeo. That love had been in his soul as well as his genes. But he didn't need to get hurt like his father and brother to quit as it turned out. He was home—following his heart.

He was the third-oldest behind Willy and James, and like his brothers he had enjoyed life on the road and made enough money to put quite a bit away. But for a while now he'd been feeling the need to grow roots. It had made him restless. When James had taken over their father's business back here in Lonesome, Tommy had felt the pull.

But that wasn't what had made the decision for him, James was right about that. He turned to face his brother. "Did you hear that Bella is back?"

James swore. "I thought you'd lost your nerve bronc riding in the rodeo," he joked. "Instead, you've lost your mind. Not Bella Worthington?"

"Afraid so," Tommy said. "She and I ran into each other in Denver a couple of weeks ago."

James opened the bottom drawer of the desk and

pulled out what was left of the bottle of blackberry brandy and two paper cups. "If this conversation about Bella is going the way I suspect it is, then we better finish this bottle." He poured. Tommy took his full paper cup, stared at it a moment before he downed it.

His brother laughed. "So maybe you do realize that what you're thinking is beyond crazy. Do I have to remind you who her father is? Not a fan of yours or the rest of us, for that matter. I'm sure he has aspirations of her marrying some biz-whiz with big bucks."

"It's not up to him," Tommy said as he smiled and traced the scar on his right temple. The scar was from when they were kids and he'd made the mistake of suggesting that Bella, being a girl, shouldn't try to cross the creek on a slippery log. She'd picked up a rock and nailed him, then she'd crossed the creek on the log. He smiled remembering that he'd been the one to slip off the dang log. Bella had come into the water to save him, though. It was what best friends did, she'd told him.

"The woman can be a firecracker," Tommy agreed. "Maybe that's why I've never gotten over her."

James shook his head. "What are you going to do? I suspect you won't get within a mile of the Worthington ranch before the shotgun comes out if her father is around." He shook his head and downed his brandy.

As he refilled the cups, his brother asked, "How'd this happen? You wake up one day and say, 'Hey, I haven't been kicked in the head by a bucking horse enough lately. I think I'll go home and see if Bella wants to marry me'?"

Tommy shrugged. "Something like that. I can't explain it. I guess I did wake up one day with this feeling." He met his brother's gaze. "I think it's meant to be. Running into her again in Denver, I suddenly knew what I wanted—what I've always wanted."

James studied him for a moment. "I just have one question. When she sends you hightailing it, are you planning to tuck your tail between your legs and leave Lonesome and Colt Investigations?"

"Nope," he said. "I'm serious about going into the business with you." He glanced around. "The way I see it, you need me maybe even worse than she does."

His brother laughed. "You're serious about the job—and Bella?"

"Dead serious," he said.

James shook his head. "Dangerous business going after Lady Worthington. That is one strong, determined woman."

Tommy grinned. "That's what I love about her. I can't seem to quit thinking about her. I think it's a sign."

"It's a sign all right," James mumbled under this breath, but he smiled and raised his cup. "Fine. You start work in the morning."

Tommy looked down at the paper cup full of blackberry brandy in his hand. But this time he took his time drinking it. Tomorrow, he would learn as much as James could teach him, start an online class and apply for his private investigator's license. He hadn't seen Bella yet, but he wanted to accomplish something before he did.

When he went out to the Worthington ranch to see her, come hell or high water, he planned to ask her to marry him. He had the ring in his pocket. As terrified as he was, he was doing this.

BELLA COULDN'T HELP being worried as she drove out to the ranch. She'd heard something in her father's tone when he'd called her in Denver and asked her to come see him at the ranch. There'd been an urgency that surprised—and concerned—her.

Maybe this wasn't about trying to get her to go into business with him. He often made her feel guilty for striking out on her own, but he knew why she'd declined. She didn't like his other partners, Edwin Fitzgerald Mattson and his son, Fitz. As generous as her father's offer had been, she'd also wanted to start her own business.

Her father had started his from the ground up. She thought he should understand why she wanted to succeed on her own. But the more she thought about it, she wondered if this visit would be about something different entirely.

"I need you to come home," her father had said.

She hadn't been back to Lonesome River Ranch in months because of her business. When he'd called, she'd given legitimate excuses as to why she couldn't come home right now.

"Bella." His voice had broken. "I have to see you. If you'd prefer that I come to you—"

"Are you sick?" she'd asked, suddenly frightened. Was it possible he was worse than sick? It seemed inconceivable. Her larger-than-life father never even got a cold.

"No. It's not that. I have to see you. I wouldn't ask, but…" His voice had broken. "I'm sorry."

"I'll come right away," she said and then hesitated before asking, "Are you there alone?"

"Except for the staff," he said, sounding both annoyed and resigned. He knew that if Edwin and Fitz were there she would refuse. The last Christmas she'd spent at the ranch had been so miserable because of the two Mattsons, she'd told her father that there would be no encore.

Parking, she got out of her vehicle in front of the ranch house and took a deep breath. The Montana summer air was ripe with the smell of pines and river. She'd missed this, another reason she was ready to make some changes.

As she started up the steps to the wide front porch that overlooked the river, her father stepped out and she felt a jolt of shock. He'd aged. While still a large, imposing man, Nolan Worthington appeared beat down, something she'd never seen before. She was instantly taken aback. He had to be sick. Her heart fell.

He quickly ushered her into the house, going straight to his den. This had always been his favorite room in the ranch house with its leather furniture, huge oak desk and small rock fireplace.

"What's wrong?" she asked, her pulse thundering with fear.

Tears filled his eyes. "I've been a fool," he said and broke down. "I'm in terrible trouble and the worst part is…" He looked up at her. "I'm afraid that I've dragged you into it."

## Chapter Three

Tommy Colt woke to sunshine—and as usual, a good strong jolt of reality. For days now, he'd been learning the investigations business from the ground up. And each morning, he'd awakened with a shock.

He'd come back to Lonesome, Montana, for a woman. A woman who had no idea how he felt and might not feel the same way. Not only had he blindly returned home for love, but he'd also quit the first and, for a long time, only love of his life. The rodeo.

Because of that, he'd thrown himself into a new job with his brother as a private detective for Colt Investigations. The two of them were following in their father's footsteps, both knowing the job had gotten Del killed.

In the light of day each morning, the whole thing seemed pretty risky on his part. But his brother

James, as Jimmy D was going by now, had already solved his first case, gotten his PI license and was making money at it. Tommy had jumped in feet-first with no training.

But then James had learned on the job when he'd decided to take over their late father's agency, he reminded himself. Clients were now pouring in.

Maybe more like trickling in, but enough so that his brother could use the help. Tommy told himself that he wanted to prove he could do this before he went out to the Lonesome River Ranch and told Bella how he felt about her. He was planning to go out to her family ranch as soon as he got settled in. He wanted to make sure he had a job and a place to live first before he asked her out on a real date, told her how he felt about her and asked her to marry him.

He had to have some experience under his belt before he told her what he'd done, quitting the job he'd had and taking on one he currently didn't know for beans. All he knew was that she'd returned to Lonesome to her family ranch—after that amazing long weekend in Denver with him. It had been platonic. That was another crazy part of this.

Tommy was planning to ask a woman he'd never even dated to marry him. What was the worst that could happen? She could say no.

James had agreed that him learning more of the business before going to see Bella was a good plan.

"I'd like to get some work out of you before you

go out there and her old man shoots you," James had said. "I doubt his feelings about you have changed."

Tommy doubted it, too. Nolan Worthington had his own aspirations for his daughter. None of those aspirations included one of the wild Colt brothers.

Since moving home, he'd found a place to live in a cabin down by the river that he could rent cheap for a while. He'd saved most of the money he'd made rodeoing. But to say his life was up in the air right now was putting it mildly.

Forcing himself out of bed, he showered and changed for work. It was an alien feeling. Could he really do a nine-to-five job?

"More manuals?" Tommy asked as he came through the door of the office later that morning. This was the most studying he'd done since college when he'd also been on the rodeo team. He figured James would start him out doing something like filing once he finished with his studies.

"I have a skip for you," James said now, shoving a sheet of paper across the desk at him without looking up.

Tommy couldn't help being surprised. "A real job?"

"What were you expecting, a soft, cushy desk job?" James laughed. "It's an easy one, Ezekiel Murray."

"Wait, *Zeke*?"

"I would imagine you'll find him downtown at the Lariat."

The Lariat bar was one of three bars in Lonesome. Like a lot of Montana towns there were more bars than churches, more pickups than cars, more Stetsons than baseball caps.

Tom checked the time as he picked up the paper, folded it and stuffed it into pocket. 8:45 a.m. If Zeke were already at the bar, it would mean one of two things—he'd been there all night, or he was starting earlier than usual. Either was trouble.

"Is this like my initiation? Bringing in Zeke?" Tom asked half-jokingly.

"I hear that he's mellowed," his brother said, still without looking up from his desk.

Tom laughed doubtfully. Even Zeke mellowed would be wilder than probably any bronc he'd tried to ride.

James looked up. "If you can't handle it…"

In the Colt family, those words were tossed out as a challenge at best. At worse, foreplay for a fistfight.

"I'm on it," Tom said as he headed for the door. This was definitely a test—just not one he'd expected. But there was no turning it down.

Colt Investigations was housed in an old two-story building along the main drag. Their father, Del, had bought the building, rented out the ground floor and used the upstairs apartment as an office.

But James was currently working on moving the office to the ground floor now that Tom was joining the business. The upstairs would remain an apartment where James was living while his house was being built on the old Colt Ranch outside of town. He and Lori, who owned the sandwich shop next door to Colt Investigations, would be getting married on the Fourth of July weekend.

"What did Zeke do this time?" Tommy asked, stopping just inside the office door before leaving.

"Drunk and disorderly, destruction of property, resisting arrest. The usual. His mother put up the bail. He missed his court hearing yesterday."

"Great," Tom said. "So all I have to do is walk him over to the jail."

James chuckled as he looked up from what he'd been working on. "Easy peasy for a guy like you."

Tommy grinned, nodding. "I knew you were jealous of how much bigger, stronger and tougher I am than you. Better looking, too."

"Yep, that's it," his brother joked. "The longer you stand here giving me a hard time, the drunker Zeke will be. Just a thought."

"Uh-huh." He put on his Stetson and strode on out the door.

It was only a little over a block to the Lariat. The town was still quiet this time of the morning. Not that there was much going on even later. Lonesome was like so many other Montana towns. Its population had dropped over time, but was now growing again as more people left the big cities for a simpler lifestyle. That was Lonesome. Simple.

He pushed open the door and was hit with the familiar smell of stale beer and floor cleaner. In the dim light, Tommy thought that this could have been any bar, anywhere in Montana. There were mounts of deer, elk, antelope and rainbow trout on the knotty-pine walls. The back bar was a warbled mirror with glowing bottles of hard liquor under canned lights.

At the end of a long scarred wooden bar sat Ezekiel Murray. His massive body teetered on a stool, body slumped forward, his huge paws wrapped around a pint of draft beer that he had just dropped a shot glass of whiskey into—shot glass and all. The whiskey was just starting to turn the beer a warm brown. Tommy would bet it wasn't his first boilermaker and would win.

In Lonesome, Zeke was known as a gentle giant—until he got a few shots in him. Tommy tried to gauge how far gone Zeke was as he approached the man.

## Chapter Four

Other than Zeke, the bar was empty except for the bartender, who was busy restocking. A newsman droned on the small television over the bar, with neither man paying any attention.

"Hey Zeke," Tommy said as he joined him.

A pair of unfocused brown eyes took him in for a moment before the man frowned. "Which one are you?"

The thing about the four Colt brothers…they all resembled each other to the point that often people didn't bother with their first names. They all had the same thick head of dark hair that usually needed cutting and blue eyes that ranged from faded denim to sky blue depending on their moods.

They were all pretty much built alike as well and all liked to think that they were the most handsome of the bunch. Close in age, they'd spent years confusing their teachers. They were simply known around the county as those wild Colt boys.

Having been gone on the rodeo circuit now for

so long, Tommy wasn't surprised that Zeke might not remember him.

"I'm Tommy Colt."

Zeke nodded, already bored by the conversation, and lifted his glass to his lips.

"I need you to take a walk with me," Tommy said standing next to Zeke's stool.

The big man looked over at him before the drink reached his lips.

"Your mother… She posted your bail."

"I don't want any trouble in here," the bartender called from a safe distance.

"Won't be any trouble," Tommy assured him. "Zeke doesn't want his mother upset. Do you, Zeke."

He wagged his big head and started to put down his drink, but then thought better of it and downed the whole thing. The shot glass that had been floating in the beer clinked against the man's teeth and rattled around the beer glass as he slurped up every drop of the booze before setting it down with a loud burp.

Okay, this probably wasn't going to go easy peasy at all, Tommy thought as Zeke got to his feet. Even at six foot four, Tommy had to look up at Zeke. And while in good shape from years of trying to ride the wildest bucking horses available, he knew he was no match for the big man.

Zeke pulled a few bills from his pocket, slapped them down on the bar and turned to Tommy. "Ready when you are."

They left the bar as the sun crested the mountains to the east. It was a beautiful summer day filled with the scent of pine from the nearby forest and that rare smell of water, sunshine and warm earth that he loved. There was nothing like a Montana summer.

Tommy couldn't believe his luck. Was it really going to be this easy? The courthouse was kitty-corner from the bar. Tommy was tempted to jaywalk, but Zeke was insistent that they walk up to the light and cross legally.

Lonesome had begun to wake up, a few cars driving past. Several honked, a couple of people waved. Tommy could just imagine what he and Zeke looked like, the gentle giant looming over the cowboy walking next to him.

The light changed. They were about to cross the street when Zeke seemed to realize where they were headed. "I thought we were going to see my ma?"

"But first we need to stop by the courthouse." The jail was right next door. Once inside, Zeke would be the deputy's problem.

"This about what I did the other night?"

"I suspect so," Tommy told him. "But once you go before the judge—"

Zeke turned so quickly Tom never saw the huge fist until it struck him in the face. He stumbled back, crashed into the front of the electronics store and sat down hard on the pavement. He could feel his right eye beginning to swell. Blinking, he looked up at Zeke.

"You realize I'm going to come after you again if you don't go peacefully with me now. Next time I'll bring a stun gun. If that isn't enough, the next time I'll bring a .45. I'm working with my brother James at Colt Investigations now and my first job was to bring you in. So, sorry, Zeke, but I gotta do it."

"I didn't say I wasn't going," Zeke said. "But I have to at least put up a fight. How would it look if I just let you take me in?" With that the man turned and walked on the crosswalk toward the courthouse.

Tommy got to his feet, only then starting to feel the pain. This was worse than getting thrown off a bucking bronco. He hurried after the man.

Once Zeke was in custody, Tommy headed back toward the office. He'd taken a ribbing from the deputies, but growing up with three brothers, he was used to abuse. He'd known this job wouldn't be easy, but so far it wasn't making him glad he quit the rodeo.

Worse, he could well imagine what James was going to say when he saw him. *Gentle giant my ass*, Tommy was thinking as he looked up and saw her. Bella Worthington.

She'd just come out of the bank and was starting to put on her sunglasses. She was crying.

"Bella?"

She hurriedly wiped the tears on her cheeks and lifted her chin, defiance in her gaze, before covering those amazing more-green-than-blue-today eyes with the sunglasses. He'd known her since they were kids playing in the woods together since their family properties were adjacent to each other.

Bella had been defiant even at a young age. Her father had forbidden her from playing with any of the Colt boys, but she'd always snuck out to meet him at the tree house they'd built together. They'd been best friends. The kind of friends that would let the other take a splinter from a finger with a pocketknife. The kind that would fight the town's worst bully even knowing the linebacker was going to kick your behind bad. The kind of friend the other would lie to protect.

"You all right?" he asked, thinking of the last time he'd seen her—just weeks ago. She'd been laughing, her head tilted back, the look in those eyes warm with emotion. They'd spent a few days and nights together, curled up on the couch in her suite at the hotel and watching old movies until they both fell asleep. They'd ordered room service breakfast and drank champagne promising that they would do it again soon.

He thought about the sweet scent of her, the way her long dark hair shone like a raven's wing, floating around her shoulders as she moved. He thought of the way she threw back her head when she laughed, exposing the tender pale flesh of her throat. And that laugh... He smiled to himself. But it was her voice he heard at night when he closed his eyes. A conspiratorial whisper next to his ear.

He and Bella had always been best as a team.

Best friends for life, he thought, touching the tiny scar on his finger that they'd cut with their pocket-knives to take their blood oath. It was as if they'd both always known how it would end, the two of them falling in love and getting married. Together forever.

Or at least that was what he'd thought, especially after their weekend in Denver. While they'd spent the time only as friends, he'd seen the promise in her eyes when she'd given him her cell phone number. "Call me. I've missed you, Tommy." She'd hesitated. "If you're going to be in Lonesome…"

He'd been surprised that she was going to the ranch and said as much. "Dad" was all she'd said with a shrug, as if it explained everything since he knew Nolan Worthington only too well. It would have something to do with business. He was always trying to get her to join him in the partnership he had with the Mattsons.

"Maybe I'll see you there," he had said, not realizing that within the next few weeks he would completely change his life for a woman he hadn't even kissed yet.

"I'm fine," Bella said now, looking embarrassed and not all that glad to see him. Even as she said it, she shook her head, denying the words out of her mouth. As her hand went to her cheek to snatch away the last fallen tear, he saw the ring and felt his eyes widen, the right one widening in pain.

"You're *engaged*?" He couldn't help his shock.

He felt gutted. She hadn't been engaged the nights they'd spent together and that was only a couple of weeks ago, or had she? *"Since when?"*

"It just happened," she said, clearly avoiding his eyes.

He shook his head, trying to make sense of this. If there'd been someone special in her life, she would have told him the weekend they were together, wouldn't she? He thought they told each other everything. Or at least used to. *"Who?"*

She cleared her throat before she spoke. He caught the slight tremor in her lips before she said, "Fitz."

He laughed and said, "That's not even funny." Of course she was joking. They'd grown up with Edwin Fitzgerald Mattson the Third. Or the *turd*, as they'd called him. Fitz had been two years older and the most obnoxious kid either of them had ever met. His father was the same way. Edwin Fitzgerald senior was Bella's father's business partner along with his son.

Because of the business arrangement, both Fitz and his father often came to the Worthington ranch. Whenever they did, Bella's father always insisted that she spend time with Fitz. But he cheated at games, threw a tantrum when he lost and told lies to get Bella into trouble if she didn't let him get his way.

Often when she knew Fitz and his father were coming to the ranch, she and Tommy would take off into the woods. They could easily outsmart Fitz as well as outrun him. Spoiled rotten, Fitz loved nothing better than making the two of them miserable. Bella had always despised Fitz, who Tommy had heard hadn't changed in adulthood.

He stared at her. "You wouldn't marry Fitz."

Anger flashed in her gaze. "Why not?"

"Because he's a jerk. Because you can't stand him. Because you can do a hell of a lot better."

"What? With someone like you?" She raised an eyebrow. "Run into a doorknob, Tommy?" she asked, indicating his right eye, which was almost swollen shut now.

"Zeke punched me, so it could be worse. Don't try to change the subject. Were you engaged when we met up in Denver?" She shook her head. "So you got engaged in the past week or so?"

She pushed her sunglasses up onto her long, dark hair and stared at him. "I don't want to talk about this with you, all right?" Instead of anger, he saw the shine of tears.

"Why would you agree to marry him?"

"Maybe he was the only one who asked," she snapped.

Tommy shook his head. "Come on, you aren't that desperate to get married or you would have asked me."

She bit her lower lip and looked away. He saw her swallow. "And what would you have said?"

"Hell yes. But that's only if you had gotten down on one knee," he added in an attempt to get things between them back like they had been not all that long ago.

Bella shook her head. "What are you doing in Lonesome? Don't you have a ride down in Texas?"

He glanced down at his boots and sighed. This certainly wasn't going the way he'd seen it in his dreams. "After we saw each other again in Denver, I came home." He met her gaze. "You said you were going to be here. I left the rodeo circuit."

"Why would you do that?" she asked, her voice breaking. She knew he'd loved being part of the family legacy. He'd been on the back of a horse from the time his father set him in a saddle while he was still in diapers and told him to hang on.

He'd grown up looking at the old Hollywood poster of his great grandfather Ransom Del Colt, the Hollywood cowboy star; his grandfather, RD Colt Jr with his Wild West show; his own father, Del Colt. Rodeo was in his blood and if anyone knew how hard it was for him to give up, it would be Bella.

He met her gaze. "Maybe after I saw you in Denver, I wanted more."

She looked away and he could see that she was fighting tears again. "You're a fool. So now you're jobless?"

Her words felt like the flick of a whip and smarted just as much. "I'm working with James at the detective agency. The eye? I brought Zeke in after he skipped out on his bond. I've applied for my PI license. I'm staying in Lonesome."

She let out a mirthless laugh. "Great job. Bucking horses trying to kill you wasn't enough? Now you're going into the detective business? Look where it got your father."

He let out a low curse of disbelief. She knew how much he'd idolized his dad, who'd started Colt Investigations after his injury. Del had never made a lot of money but he'd helped a whole lot of people.

"I can't believe you would really go there, Bella, especially after all these years of being contemptuous of your father using money to control you."

"I'm supposed to be happy about you going into a business that got your father killed?" she snapped, sounding close to crying. "But it's your life."

"Right, and you're marrying Fitz, so what do you care?" Her chin rose in defiance. "What exactly is he offering you?"

"You wouldn't understand," she said and shifted on her feet as she slid the sunglasses back over her eyes and looked down the street away from him.

"Looking for your fiancé?" he asked. "I suspect Fitz wouldn't want you anywhere near me."

"You're right, Tommy. The best thing is for you to stay away from me." Her voice broke and he saw her throat work as if she'd wished she'd swallowed her words rather than let them fly out like she had.

"Wow, the difference a couple of weeks can make," he said as he took a step back. "I sure misread that weekend with you. Maybe a whole lifetime spent together. Guess I didn't know you as well as

I thought. I take it back. Fitz is perfect for you." He started to turn away.

*"Tommy?"*

He heard the tearful plea, felt her fingers brush his sleeve and he stopped to look back at her. What he saw in her expression nearly dropped him to his knees. Just then he saw Fitz appear behind her, all decked out in a three-piece suit that probably cost more than Tommy's horse. The man didn't look happy to see him talking to Bella, but Fitz's displeasure was nothing compared to Tommy's.

"Good luck," he said to Bella and turned away before he put his fist in Fitz's face. He felt shock and disappointment and an unbearable sense of loss as he walked away. He and Bella had had something special. He was sure of that. Why would she agree to marry Fitz? It was inconceivable, especially after the two of them had been together just like the old days merely weeks ago. It wasn't possible that in that period of time she'd gotten engaged. And yet he'd seen the large diamond on her finger. He'd heard the words come out of her mouth.

So why was he still unable to believe it?

He slowed his steps. He kept thinking about the last look that Bella had given him in Denver. Could the woman change her mind that quickly? Especially a woman he'd known all his life. He thought of the hours they'd spent in their tree house. They'd shared their secrets, they'd shared their desires, they'd even shared their blood with their prized

pocketknives. He thought of the two of them together in Denver. That lifetime connection was still
there—only stronger.

He stopped and looked back. Fitz put his arm
around Bella, but she pulled away only to have him
grab her hand and jerk her roughly back toward
him. Lovers' quarrel? Or something else?

He caught a glimpse of Bella's face. Something
was wrong. He knew this woman. She wasn't acting like a woman in love.

## Chapter Five

Bella was still shaken when she reached her car after seeing Tommy—only to be accosted by her so-called fiancé. Fitz. She hated everything about him. The way he brushed back his blond hair with that arrogant shake of his head. She really hated that smug expression that marred an otherwise hand-some face. He was strong and fit. No doubt he had a trainer who kept him that way. But he wasn't agile. Even as a kid, he couldn't climb a tree or jump a ditch or run fast enough to catch her.

He'd always been a bully and that hadn't changed. She shoved away that image of the pudgy Edwin Fitzgerald Mattson. The man she was dealing with now was much more formidable.

Looks were everything to Fitz. Like his car, his fancy condo in the city, his gold jewelry he seemed so fond of. She'd caught the glint of a few inches of gold chain at his neck. It must have been new be-cause he kept reaching up to touch it as if to make sure it was still there.

But it was that self-satisfied look on his face that had made her want to attack him on the street, her hatred of him growing by the hour. The problem was she didn't know how she was ever going to beat him at his own game. He had her neck in a half nelson and wasn't about to let go until he got what he wanted.

She warned herself that she had to keep her cool and pretend she was going through with this ridiculous wedding that Fitz was planning. He had invited everyone in the county. He was so sure that there was nothing she could do to get out of it.

The only way she could keep from losing her mind was by telling herself she was merely stalling for time. She would get this sorted out. She would see that her father's name was cleared so Fitz could no longer blackmail her—or die trying.

Just the thought of Fitz made her stomach roil. Worse was the thought of Tommy Colt because that made her want to sit down and bawl her eyes out. He was right. She was in love with him. She'd been from as far back as she could remember. He'd been her bestie. He'd been her everything growing up.

Her father had been immersed in his business. When Nolan was around, so was his partner and Fitz. It was no wonder that she preferred the company of wild boy Tommy Colt and his equally feral brothers. They'd been her true family.

Now, as she drove toward the ranch, she knew that feeling sorry for herself wasn't doing her any good. She had to figure out what to do next—and quickly. She'd never felt more alone. Or more scared. The clock was ticking, the wedding coming up fast.

Looking down at the pretentious huge diamond ring on her finger, she wanted to rip if off and throw it out the window. But what would that accomplish? She had to help her father. Losing her temper would only make matters worse.

TOMMY WATCHED BELLA and Fitz part at her vehicle. Clearly angry, Fitz drove off in an obnoxious mustard-yellow sports car, the tires smoking. Bella sat in her SUV for a few minutes before leaving as well. He recalled that she'd been crying as she came out of the bank. He knew what it took to make Bella cry.

What had happened inside the bank? Was it about Fitz? Or something else? He had to find out what was going on and felt better as he turned back to the bank, even though his right eye was now almost swollen shut. He'd finished his first job for the detective agency. Now it was time for him to start believing that he could do this work.

Having grown up here, Tommy knew most everyone. One foot in the door of the bank and he spotted a young woman in one of the glass-wall offices. Carla Richmond had long black hair and large brown eyes. One of his brothers had dated her for a while, though he couldn't remember which one.

He stuck his head into her office doorway. "Have a minute?"

After her initial surprise, he could see her trying to figure out which one he was. "It's Tommy," he said as he stepped in and closed the door behind him. "I could use your help."

It was clear that Carla thought he'd come in for a bank loan. She started to reach for an application form, but he stopped her as he took a chair in front of her desk.

"This is awkward," he said, leaning forward. "I wouldn't ask but it's important. It's about Bella. Bella Worthington?"

She nodded and carefully replaced the form she'd been about to hand him. "You realize that I can't talk about—"

"She left here crying."

"I'm sorry to hear that," Carla said carefully.

"I don't want specifics, okay? I just need to know what might have caused the tears." He saw her jaw set. "Her father's rich. I would think she would come out of a bank all smiles." He caught that slight change in her expression. Something in those dark eyes. He felt a start.

"Tommy, you know I can't talk to you about bank business." She started to stand.

"Please, just tell me if you know why Bella was crying." He put his hand over his heart. "She means everything to me."

She sat back down and shook her head, but he

could feel her weakening. "How is your brother Davy?" she finally asked as if changing the subject.

So it was Davy she was interested in. "He's still rodeoing, but I suspect it won't be long and he'll be coming home. You want me to let him know that you asked after him?"

She started to shake her head but stopped. "I suppose. If it comes up. We dated for a while in high school."

He smiled at her. "That's right. Look, how about you say nothing and I just run some thoughts past you." Before she could argue, he went on. "I doubt Bella is having any financial problems. Her business is going great guns from what she'd told me."

Carla's expression confirmed it.

"So who does that leave?" Again, that quick flicker in her eyes. He frowned. "Her father? Is he ill?" Tommy would have heard. Bella would have mentioned it. It dawned on him what Carla was *not* saying.

He let out a curse. It was a bank, not a hospital. "It's financial to do with her father." She looked past him again, clearly nervous. He could tell by her pained expression that he'd guessed it. "He's in financial trouble?"

She avoided his gaze as she rose and stood with her palms pressed to the top of her desk. "As I said—"

"I get it. You can't tell me." Tommy stood up. "I'll take one of those loan forms if you don't mind."

Carla looked relieved as she pulled out one and handed it to him. "I didn't tell you anything. Not a word."

He nodded. "Thanks." He held up the form. "I'll tell Davy I saw you."

Was it possible that Nolan Worthington was in financial trouble? If so, it would certainly explain what Bella was doing back in Lonesome at the ranch. With a curse, he realized it could also explain why she had agreed to marry Fitz. He thanked Carla and left her office.

He had to see Bella again.

But first he needed his brother's help.

James looked up from his desk and grinned as Tommy came into the office. "Nice eye. Zeke?"

"Good guess." He pulled the signed, delivered form from his pocket and tossed it on his brother's desk.

James picked it up, saw what it was and blinked. "I thought that might be your resignation letter."

"I told you, I'm in this all the way. We have a new case."

His brother lifted a brow. "A paying case?"

Tommy shrugged and pulled up a chair in front of his brother's desk. "If you don't agree it's a case we should take, well then I'll pay for it as your new partner."

"I'm not sure you understand how the business works," James said as he leaned back in his chair, but Tommy could tell that he was intrigued. He quickly told him about running into Bella as she was coming out of the bank crying.

"She's engaged to Fitz!" James shook his head. "I thought you said you and she—"

"Exactly." He told him about their conversation and then about Fitz showing up and the two arguing on the street. "I could tell something was wrong so I went into the bank. Did you know Carla Richmond works there?"

"Davy's old girlfriend. They were pretty serious back in high school."

"Right, anyway, she couldn't divulge anything about bank business..."

"But you got it out of her." James was sitting forward now, clearly interested.

"It's Nolan Worthington. He's in financial trouble."

James blinked. "Bad investments?"

"I don't know. It still doesn't make any sense. Why would a self-made man who went from nothing to filthy rich be so stupid as to make bad investments?"

"Is the partnership in trouble or just him?" James asked.

"No idea." He hadn't even thought of that. Maybe his brother was a better investigator than any of them had thought—and the one big cold case he solved wasn't a fluke.

James opened his computer and started to type, then abruptly stopped. "Wait. You were just with her in Denver. She didn't mention any of this, including the engagement?"

"She wasn't engaged but she said she'd gotten a call from her father and was headed for the ranch. She didn't sound happy about it. Something is wrong for her to even consider marrying Fitz." James looked away. "What?" Tommy demanded, knowing the look all too well.

"I didn't want to be the one to say it, but…" James looked up. "Maybe she's marrying Fitz because her dad's in trouble financially."

"I already thought of that, but we're talking about Bella. She isn't like that."

When James raised a brow, Tommy swore, wanting to cuff his brother upside the head for not believing him. "Then how do you explain it?" James finally said. "Did you ask her?"

Tommy sighed, got up and walked over to the Hollywood poster of his grandfather. Her being engaged to Fitz made no sense. Was it possible this woman he'd loved for so long was that shallow? Had he been a fool to quit the rodeo and come back here?

He turned back to his brother. "She said Fitz was the only one who'd asked."

"You think she's just trying to get you to step up?" James asked.

Tommy shook his head. "She knows how I feel about her. Even if I haven't spelled it out, this engagement is too sudden. Knowing what I do know about her father, I have to help her."

"That's just it," James said. "You don't know anything for certain. You need facts."

"You're right," he said as he came back over to the desk. "I need to find out the truth—with your help, bro. I need a quick course in PI."

"Then pull up a chair and let's see what we can find out about Nolan Worthington and his business and partners, Edwin Fitzgerald Mattson and his obnoxious son, Fitz."

THAT FIRST DAY BACK AT the ranch, Bella had been forced to drag the sorry tale out of her father. He'd said he hadn't been paying enough attention to what was going on with the business. Edwin had him sign papers all the time. He hadn't thought anything about it.

"What did he get you into?" she demanded. She'd never trusted Edwin Mattson let alone his son Fitz, who was now invested in the business.

Her father shook his head. "I'm in trouble. The Feds are involved. I have no proof that I didn't do any of it. But these businesses it says I bought? They're money laundering operations." He broke down, dropping his face into his hands. "I sold them as soon as I realized what I'd apparently done, but I lost so much money and the Feds are even more interested in me now."

She had to pull every sorry word out of him, but she quickly got a picture of what Fitz had done to him. He'd tricked her father, who hadn't realized that at least Fitz—and maybe his father as well—had set him up to take away the business Nolan had started. Of course, if he were arrested on a felony, he would be forced out of the business he'd started.

"It's worse than even that," her father said. "Fitz says he has proof that I've been embezzling from the company for the past six months for my drug habit. I'm sure that if any money is missing, it's been going into his pocket. But while none of that is true, added to the mistakes I've made…"

"You look guilty." He was also acting guilty, she noted. "So basically they're about to fleece you," she said and frowned. "You've hired a good lawyer, right?"

He looked at the floor. "I made a bad investment. I'm afraid I'm broke. It's all gone. Everything but this ranch and now I'm headed for prison."

Her hatred for Edwin and his son had her pacing the den in fury. "Surely you have some recourse."

He lowered his head, shaking it slowly. "The judge usually goes easy on a first-time offender—if I agree to pay back the money, but that's impossible. On top of that, now with the Feds… Edwin and Fitz have been setting me up for months." He met her gaze. "They have our investors believing I have a drug problem. A few months ago at a restaurant I was drugged and appeared…" He broke down again. "There'd been rumors going around about me, I guess, started by them. I found drugs in the glove box of my car and got rid of them, but

I never know where drugs are going to turn up. They have me tied up. There is nothing I can do."

Her blood boiled, but she knew she had to keep her head. One of them had to be strong right now. "There must be a way to prove that this is all a setup." She stared at her father. It couldn't be possible. There was no way the man she'd known all her life was taking this lying down. Nolan Worthington had gotten where he'd been by being smart and doggedly determined. He'd built the business that Edwin and Fitz were now stealing from him. "There has to be something we can do."

His gaze lifted to hers. She caught hope in his green eyes so much like her own. "Fitz said he can make it all go away."

She waited, knowing that whatever her father said next would be bad. She just didn't know how bad. "What do you have to do?" she asked in a whisper.

"Fitz has been taking over his father's part of the company for some time now. He's the one who's in control, according to Edwin. If so, Fitz has me right where he wants me. You know he's always been jealous of what I built, this ranch—"

"What is it Fitz wants?" she demanded, fear edging her voice. She knew Fitz, knew the kind of boy he'd been, the kind of man he'd grown into. "What?"

Nolan Worthington held her gaze tremulously. "You. He wants you."

She shook her head and took a step back, too

shocked to speak for a moment. "Well, he can't have me."

Her father nodded in resignation. "I can't say I blame you."

They both went silent for a long moment. "What happens if he doesn't get his way?" she finally asked, remembering the deplorable child she'd known.

Nolan Worthington looked away. "It doesn't matter. I can't ask you—"

"Tell me." She waited.

He finally looked at her again. His eyes filled with tears. "This isn't your problem. I got myself into this and—"

"Tell me what happens if he doesn't get me."

"He'll send me to prison," her father said. "He'll plant more drugs. He'll see that I get the maximum time. Twenty years."

Twenty years. A life sentence at his age. She swallowed and said, "Fitz is going to have to say that to my face."

"You won't have to wait long. He said he plans to meet you here at the ranch." Her father pulled himself together. "I need to tell the staff. He's replacing them all and basically kicking everyone out but you—even if you agree to marry him. I'd rather let them go than have him do it."

"Wait, he can't just take over the ranch. You said it's in my name."

Her father stared at the floor. "He said he plans to stay here until the wedding and if you didn't like it, you could discuss it with me in my jail cell."

Bella was unable to speak. If Fitz thought he could bully her… But even as she realized it, she knew that it wasn't an idle threat.

Her father stumbled to his feet and reached for her. "I knew I had to tell you what was going on. I'm so sorry, but I can't ask you to—" He hugged her and she felt him trembling.

"And if I do this?" she asked, her anger making her blood thunder through her veins.

He let go of her to step back so he could see her face. She saw a glimmer of the father she'd known flash in his eyes as anger. "Then he will produce evidence that proves I'm innocent. He said he'd even buy my share of the business. I'm sure he will do it for pennies on the dollar, but at least I won't be in prison."

She wasn't able to believe this. "How can he make this all go away just like that?" she demanded with a snap of her fingers.

"Apparently he has another scapegoat."

Bella stared at him. "His father?"

"I don't know. Maybe this was Edwin's idea."

She shook her head wondering if her father really believed that. "So what do you get if I go along with this?"

"I'd be out of the company," he said. "But Fitz will pay me enough that I could live comfortably, but only if I left the country since my reputation is ruined, thanks to the two of them. Even with proof, no one will believe I wasn't guilty."

## Chapter Six

As threatened, Fitz had arrived a few days after Bella's return to Lonesome. He'd driven up in his expensive yellow sports car—one that verged on ridiculous in this part of Montana. He'd be lucky if he didn't break an axle on the ranch road. Come winter, he'd high center the car in the deep snow and freeze to death. She could only hope.

Bella had warned herself not to lose her temper. It wouldn't help her father even though she knew it would make her feel better.

Fitz shook back his mop of blond hair to expose small blue eyes the color of twilight. He had that same haughty look on the classically handsome face that he had as a boy. It said, *I'm spoiled rotten and hateful and there is nothing you can do about it.*

She feared this time he was right as she opened the door before he reached it. She'd called him days earlier, wanting him to confirm what he'd told her father—and record the conversation. He'd ignored the calls.

He stopped, a smirk coming to his lips as he pushed his sunglasses up onto his head and met her gaze. Bella thought she could have started a fire with the heat radiating out of her eyes. For a moment, he didn't look quite so sure of himself.

"I'm assuming you talked to your father," he said as he looked around, clearly avoiding her laser gaze.

"My phone messages weren't clear enough for you?"

His gaze came back to her along with the smirk. He raised an eyebrow. "You called me?"

She said nothing, waiting. Let the bastard admit what he'd done. She had her hand around her cell in the pocket of her pants, her finger hovering over Record.

He finally looked at her again. "I suppose he told you. Damned shame. Your dad should have known better."

That she could agree on. She'd never liked him going into business with Edwin Fitzgerald Mattson even before Fitz got involved. There was something about the man that she hadn't trusted—even as a child.

"So now what?" Fitz asked, getting visibly annoyed to be left standing outside the lodge. Had he really expected to be invited in?

"You tell me."

"At least invite me in. After all, pretty soon this ranch will be mine." He laughed and started up the steps toward her. "Excuse me, *ours*. It will all be ours."

"Over your dead body," she said, making him stop in midstep.

He raised an eyebrow, his mouth quirking into a smirk. "I thought your father would have told you how much trouble he's in. I hope you have the money for a good lawyer for him. He's going to need it. My father and I were shocked when we found out what he's been doing behind our backs."

She couldn't believe Fitz would lie like this to her face. Then again, she knew she shouldn't be surprised. She said as much, daring him to tell the truth for once. His expression suddenly changed as if he realized what she was up to.

He came at her, grabbing her arm and pulling her hand from her pocket with the cell still clutched in it. With a laugh, he pried the phone from her fingers. "You said you wanted to talk, when you left me all those messages."

"So you did get my messages," she said. "Too bad you didn't take any of them to heart."

"Threatening my life?" He shook his head. "You are only adding fuel to the fire. Like father, like daughter."

What made her even angrier was that he was right. She needed to keep a clear head and find a way out of this. Threats were a waste of time. But it would be next to impossible not to want to claw his eyes out.

"If anything, you should be nice to me," he said smiling broadly. "It's to your advantage."

"I wouldn't count on that," she snapped, unable to hold her tongue.

His blue eyes, a deep navy, darkened even further as he gave her a push back into the open doorway.

It was all she could do not to physically push back. She feared what would happen though if she could get her hands around his neck. But he was right. He had the upper hand. At least for the moment. She took a step back and then another, afraid of what she would do if he shoved her again. She needed time to try to find a way out of this. She wasn't letting her father go to prison. But she also wasn't marrying this fool.

Once in her father's study, Fitz closed the door. "I could use a drink. How about you?" he asked as he walked to the bar.

"A little early in the day for me." He went to her father's bar as if he owned the place. Apparently he would soon enough unless she could stop him.

"Where's the help?" Fitz asked as he turned from the bar, a full drink in his hand. "There's no ice in the bucket."

Since her father normally lived in an apartment near his office in Missoula, there had been only part-time staff at the ranch except during the months he came here to stay. "My father let the staff all go as per your instructions apparently," she said. It was hard to be civil to this man. But she'd try a white flag of surrender first. If she didn't get the information she needed, she'd resort to all-out war.

Fitz chuckled. "I think that is the first time Nolan has ever done anything I asked him to do." He smiled. "How times change."

She watched him take a slug of his drink, lick his lips and settle his gaze on her again before she asked, "Your idea of a marriage proposal is to frame my father?"

He had the good grace to drop his gaze to the floor for a moment. "Over the years, I've tried other approaches."

"I recall. Slamming me against a file cabinet to grope my breast. Cornering me in the kitchen and spilling your drink down the front of my blouse as you forcibly tried to kiss me."

"'Forcibly' is a tad dramatic," he snapped. "I've tried nicely to get your attention. I decided on a different approach after you rebuffed my every advance."

"You could have just gotten the message and backed off."

His gaze hardened to ice chips. "I don't want to back off. In case you didn't get the message, I want you and I will use any measures to have what I want."

She nodded. "Just like when you were a boy and didn't get your way. This is just another form of tantrum." She turned and walked to the window so he couldn't see how hard she was shaking. None of this was going to help her father. If anything, Fitz would tighten the screws.

Bella turned to look at him again. It was all she could do not to gag at the sight of him slurping down her father's expensive bourbon. She could never let him win, for her father, for the ranch she loved, but mostly for her own sake. She swore right then, she would kill him before she ever became this man's wife.

"What now?" she asked trying to keep the tremor out of her voice.

He smiled as if he thought she'd finally accepted the inevitable. "We get married. Didn't your father tell you that I want the whole package? A big wedding. I've already sent out invitations to most of the county. It's going to be in the barn here at the ranch. It's going to be till death us do part."

She nodded, thinking she could live with the death part. "I really can't see you married to anyone, let alone me."

He put down his empty glass and stepped toward her. She stood her ground even as the floor seemed to quake under her. Reaching into his pocket he pulled out a velvet box and shoved it toward her.

She didn't take it, didn't move. Instead, she looked down at the floor. Fitz was simple and spoiled, but he wasn't entirely stupid.

He let out a sigh. "Fine. We can do it your way if that's what will make you happy." She watched him drop to one knee and thought since he was already on the floor how easily it would have been to end this right now. One good kick with her cowboy boot and he would be helplessly writhing on the floor. But it wouldn't help her father if she went to prison as well right now.

"Bella Alexandria Worthington, I'm asking for your hand in marriage," he said with a sigh and opened the box.

The diamond engagement was gaudy and ridiculously ostentatious. She looked from it to him. "It looks exactly like something you would choose." If he caught the sarcasm, he didn't show it.

"Only the biggest and best for you," he said and took the ring from the box and reached for her hand.

She thought of her father and tamped down her fury. Was she really going to let this man blackmail her into becoming his fiancée? If she hoped to stall for time to figure a way out of this, she had to at least let him think she was.

She stuck her hand into his face and he put the ring on her finger. It surprised her that it almost fit. He must have found out her ring size. She met his gaze, wondering what else he'd found out about her. That she'd been with Tommy recently for an entire weekend? It wouldn't matter that they hadn't made love. Fitz had always been jealous of the closeness she and Tommy had shared over the years.

As Fitz awkwardly got to his feet, she realized how dangerous this man was. What he'd done to her father was diabolical. All because she'd spurned his advances?

Bella looked down at the ring on her finger. Maybe this was just a show of power. He wanted her to know that he was in control. He didn't really want to tie himself to a woman who couldn't stand the sight of him, did he?

"Why would you want to marry me?" she asked quietly.

The question seemed to take him by surprise. "Have you looked in the mirror lately?" he asked with a laugh. "I want other men to look at me with naked jealousy."

"I saw your sports car. You can have any woman you want, women who are better looking than me. So why me?"

"Because I can and because you and I are the same." She instantly wanted to argue against that, but he didn't give her a chance. "Bella, you go after what you want. Look at the way you turned your father down when you had a chance to go into business with him."

"With you and your father you mean."

He smiled. "Yes, with me. That was a mistake. You should have joined the partnership and not forced me to take other measures." He was blaming her for this? "You and I could own the world."

"I don't want to own the world," she said and swallowed back the bile that rose in her throat. The conceit of this man, the hollowness of his desires, his all-out criminal behavior, and for what? Just to feed his ego?

"Well, you'll be with me soon and I want to own the world any way I can get it," he said.

"I can see that." He seemed to take her words as a compliment until he looked into her eyes.

"You may not like my methods. Fight me all you want, but I'd hate you to have to visit your father in prison. That is, if he doesn't overdose before then. Or jump out a window from our office building. Desperate men do desperate things."

Her hands knotted into fists at her side. She heard the threat and knew it wasn't idle. It was all she could do not to lunge for his throat.

"As your fiancé I'll be moving into the ranch right away since the wedding is going to be here and it's coming up soon. Your large new barn is the perfect place for the wedding, don't you think?"

She shook her head. "You're not moving in here."

Fitz moved swiftly for a man of his size. "When are you going to realize that you no longer have a say in anything?" He grabbed her by the waist and pulled her into a kiss. She bit his lip, making him howl. He took a step back and slapped her so hard her ears rang, but he didn't try to touch her again.

As he'd gone back to the bar, Bella had promised herself that Fitz would never be her husband. One way or another, she would stop this marriage.

## Chapter Seven

Tommy pulled up a chair as his brother began to type at his computer. "Let's see what we can find out." He watched James go to a variety of sites, taking notes, determined to learn as much as he could quickly.

"This is interesting," James said. "Six months ago, Nolan bought some small businesses. During those six months, he'd gone through a lot of money on top of what appears to be several bad investments."

"So he is broke?"

"This does not look good. Car washes are cash-heavy businesses like casinos and strip clubs. Simply owning businesses like that is a red flag for the Feds. This could get him investigated for money laundering even though it appears that he turned around and sold them quickly at a loss, which frankly I would think makes him look even more guilty."

"You think he's involved in money laundering?" Tommy asked in surprise.

James lifted an eyebrow and shrugged. "The thing is, in most business partnerships, if one of the partners is arrested for a felony, the remaining partners can buy him out for pennies on the dollar."

"So you're saying that Nolan Worthington could lose everything."

"It certainly looks that way," his brother said. "I always thought he was a smart businessman. Didn't he start the investment business from the ground up? No wonder Bella's upset." James began to type again on the keyboard. "But at least it looks as if the ranch is in her name. That's good."

"Until she marries Fitz," Tommy said. "Then he'd own fifty percent should there be a divorce." Tommy thought about the ranch that Bella loved. She wouldn't jeopardize it to save her father, would she? "How did this happen?" He knew he was asking why Bella would have ever agreed to marry Fitz under any circumstances.

"Greed? The business with Edwin Mattson seems to be doing fine," James said. "Maybe Nolan wanted to make more money. Maybe he got involved with the wrong people." He seemed to hesitate. "I did hear a rumor that he might have gotten involved with drugs."

Tommy shook his head. "Nolan? That's not possible."

James shrugged. "Fitz started his own business

no doubt financed by his father. He's doing fine. Didn't Bella start her own business?"

He nodded. "But she's barely gotten it off the ground. She wouldn't have the funds to bail out her father."

James closed his computer. "Could explain why she's agreed to marry Fitz, though."

Tommy wanted to argue that James didn't know Bella the way he did. She'd never marry Fitz under any circumstances, let alone marry any man for money. But there was that huge rock he'd seen on her ring finger. Not to mention the words out of her mouth. He stood and shoved back the extra chair. "I've got to talk to Bella."

BELLA KNEW THAT she had to move quickly after Fitz's visit. The wedding day he had chosen was coming up fast. She realized that her father hadn't really explained how Fitz had left him so bankrupt. Conning him out of the partnership was one thing. What about her father's other investments? He shouldn't be this broke.

She called Fitz's father, wondering what kind of reception she would get. Edwin senior had always been kind to her even though she'd never trusted him. But when it came to Fitz, Edwin had almost been apologetic. Had that changed? Surely he was aware what Fitz was up to.

"Edwin, it's Bella," she said when he answered his phone at the office. For a moment all she heard was silence on the other end. "I'm sure you know why I'm calling. There's a few things I need to know. Starting with my father's finances."

There was a deep sigh. "This is something you should be asking your father."

"I'm asking you," she said, hating that underlying regret she heard in the man's voice as well as the pleading in her own. "Please. There is so much going on right now with Fitz… Tell me why my father's broke." She could understand Fitz and Edwin using the clause in the partnership to get him out of the business. But there had to be more going on here.

Edwin cleared his throat. "Apparently you are unaware of your father's indiscretions."

"Indiscretions?"

The man sounded embarrassed. "You really should take this up with your father."

"I would but I don't know what *this* is," she said losing her patience.

"Ask him about Caroline."

The name meant nothing to her.

"That's all I can tell you. I'm so sorry." Edwin disconnected.

Bella knew he could tell her much more, but he wasn't going to. Apparently she would have to hear it straight from the horse's mouth. How much more had her father kept from her?

He had gone back to his apartment in Missoula, which was only blocks from his office. She'd been so busy starting her online Western wear business that she hadn't been to his apartment since he'd first rented it. Instead, what little she'd seen of him had been at the ranch—usually at his request. Now she wondered if that was because he kept this Caroline at the apartment.

On the drive to Missoula, she had too much time to think about all of this. As she reached the new high-rise apartment house and parked, that stupid engagement ring on her finger caught the light, winking at her as if in on the ruse. She took it off and tossed it into her purse.

Her father's SUV was in the lot, but when she reached the reception area on the lower floor, the man behind the desk wasn't going to let her go up.

"He's had movers in and out all day," the man dressed in a security uniform told her. "Other residents are complaining about him tying up the elevator."

"You can take it up with him," she said. "I'm his daughter and I'm going up to see him."

The man looked as if he wanted to argue. "Fine, but please tell your father that the movers he hired need to use the service elevator."

Her father was moving? So much for her theory that he was keeping this Caroline woman in the apartment. But where was he moving? Surely not back to the ranch. Or was he preparing for prison? she thought with a sense of panic as she took the elevator up to his floor and rang his doorbell.

Her father opened the door, clearly surprised to see her after their discussion at the ranch a few days ago. She was equally surprised to find him in such disarray. He hadn't shaved for a couple of days and appeared to be wearing the same clothes he'd had on the last time she'd seen him.

Past him, the apartment was filled with boxes. She caught the scent of old takeout and saw the food containers discarded on the breakfast bar along with several nearly empty alcohol bottles before she closed the door behind her and stepping past him. Her father never drank much, just a nightcap of his precious bourbon—not the rot-gut stuff that had been in the discarded liquor bottles she was seeing.

"I haven't had time to pick up," he said, stepping to the breakfast bar and beginning to toss items into the trash.

She moved deeper into the apartment. "What is going on?"

He stopped cleaning up, seeming surprised. "I already told you."

"You apparently left out a few things," she said. "Who is Caroline?"

All the blood drained from his face. He planted a hand on the breakfast bar as if to steady himself. "Who…who told—"

"It doesn't matter who told me."

"Fitz? Or his father?"

She'd never seen Nolan Worthington look more defeated. She wanted to reach for him and assure him that they would get through this. Except she didn't know the extent of what this was. But from the look on his face, this was even worse than what he'd told her before. "What have you done?"

He bristled and straightened taking on the stature of the father she'd always known. "I'd appreciate you not using that tone with me." She waited. "Could we at least sit down?"

She looked around for a place to sit, moved a couple of half-packed boxes and sat. He went to the breakfast bar. Picked up one of the almost empty bottles of bourbon and poured what there was into a dirty glass.

"I'd offer you one but…" He drained the glass, then came into the living area, moved a box and sat down some distance from her. The alcohol put a little color back into his face. "I made a mistake. It happens."

Bella sighed. How many mistakes had he made? Even more than he'd admitted to so far. "Just tell me so we can deal with it."

His Adam's apple bobbed for a moment before he spoke. "I met a woman. Caroline Lansing. I… I fell in love with her."

"She took all your money." It was a wild guess, but she saw at once that she'd hit a bull's-eye on the first try even as she told herself that her father was too smart to be swindled by a gold-digging woman. But he'd been alone for years since her mother's death. Lonely men could be easy prey for a female with criminal designs.

And Bella hadn't been around. "How bad is it?" She knew it had to be very bad.

"She… I…thought we were getting married. She let me believe that she had money, but that it was tied up in real estate, so I…" He shook his head. He didn't need to continue.

"She's long gone?" He nodded. "With your money?" Another nod. "None of that matters right now," he snapped. "Fitz is trying to put me in prison."

When she said nothing, he added, "Go ahead and say it. I was stupid. I was played for a fool." His voice broke. "I was in love for the second time in my life."

Bella didn't know what to say. There really wasn't anything she could say. "Is there nothing left?"

"Just the ranch."

She had a feeling that her father would have probably raided the ranch for this woman if he hadn't legally put it in his daughter's name. She would bet money Caroline, whoever she was, had wanted every last cent he had and would have gotten the ranch if she could have.

"So this is why you're broke, this woman? Do you have any way to get your money back from her, legally or otherwise?" she asked.

He shook his head. "It's gone. She's gone."

"How long did you know her?"

"I met her six months ago," he said. "I was… distracted and Fitz took advantage."

Six months. Was that when Fitz began plotting to destroy both her father and her? Bella glanced around at all the boxes. "Where are moving to?"

"Everything is going into storage." He met her gaze. "My life is so up in the air, and I can't come back to the ranch. I know Fitz is moving in."

"That's what he says." She had much bigger problems. If she didn't marry Fitz, her father would be going to jail and then prison. Even if she did marry Fitz, her father's future was still uncertain. He was broke. Fitz was threatening to enforce the breach of contract clause in the partnership so that her father would lose everything, including his reputation.

"How did you meet this woman?" Bella asked.

"She came to the office, wanted advice on an investment," he said sheepishly. "One thing led to another."

She didn't doubt that Fitz had taken advantage of her father being distracted by this woman. But she couldn't help being suspicious that he'd been set up, and not just by Caroline. It seemed odd that the woman just happened to be sent back to her father's office.

"Do you have a photo of her?" Bella asked.

Her father looked surprised. Who kept a photo of the woman who had fleeced him? A man who'd truly believed he'd been in love. He started to reach for his cell phone.

"Send it to me and everything you know about her." She got to her feet. Her father looked better than when he'd opened the door. He had raised a strong, resourceful, smart daughter. However, she doubted even she could save him from himself. But she would try because he was her father.

She kissed him on the cheek as she left. The tears she'd seen in his eyes made her hate Fitz even more than she thought possible because all her instincts told her that he'd had something to do with everything that Nolan Worthington was now going through—and her as well.

FITZ STOOD ON the steps of the ranch house, considering what he would do with the place once it was his. Once Bella was his. He touched his tongue to his lip where she'd bitten him. Anger made him see red. Once they were married, she was in for a rude awakening.

He'd moved up the wedding from the original date he'd planned, anxious to teach her how things were going to be. That was if he could wait that long. She would soon be his in every way whether she liked it or not.

Smiling to himself, he realized that he wouldn't mind if she fought back. It might make taking her all the more enjoyable. He knew it would be an even bigger thrill to get her on her knees than the excitement and joy he felt when he took over businesses and crushed the life out of them.

A truck pulled up out front. He saw it was from the locksmith shop in town. An elderly man climbed out. "You the one who needs the locks changed?" the man asked, glancing around. "Where's Nolan?"

"He's away on business. He asked me to take care of it. Unfortunately, I'm locked out."

The locksmith looked wary.

"I'm Edwin Fitzgerald Mattson the Third. My father and I are Nolan's business partners." At least for the moment. "Bella's my fiancée."

The man didn't move. "Where's Bella? Going to need either her or her father before I change the locks."

Fitz was about to let out a string of curses when he heard a vehicle approaching. With relief he saw it was Bella. He wondered where she'd been. He was going to have to clip her wings. She couldn't just come and go without a word to him about where she was going, but one step at a time. Clearly, she needed more convincing about who was in control here.

"Here's Bella now," he said, seething inside at how she'd locked him out of the ranch house. He really needed to bring this woman to heel and soon, he thought, narrowing his eyes at her as she climbed from her SUV. And he knew exactly how to do it.

"I understand you want the locks changed," the elderly locksmith said to her as she approached.

Bella glanced from the man to him. Her look was so defiant that for a moment Fitz worried that she would embarrass him in front of this old man.

"Oscar," she said, turning to smile at the lock-smith. "I appreciate you coming all the way out here." She turned to Fitz. The challenge in her eyes sent a spike of pure fury straight to his gut where it began to roil. So help her, if she defied him on this—

"Let me open the door, Oscar, so you can get the work done and be on your way. I know that you like to have lunch with your wife. How is Naomi doing these days?"

"She's fine, thank you for asking, Bella." Oscar grabbed his toolbox from his pickup and started up the steps after her.

As the man passed Fitz, he didn't even give him a glance. "I have some wedding arrangements to take care of," Fitz said from between clenched teeth. "I'll see you later." Not that either Bella or Oscar was listening. Bella was busy offering the locksmith a glass of iced tea for when he finished the job.

Fitz was almost to town when he realized his mistake. What were the chances Bella would give him one of the new keys? He swore, slamming his palm against the steering wheel. He should have stuck around until he had the key. She thought she was so much smarter than him and always had.

He considered what he would do if she locked him out again. It was time to teach that woman how things were going to be from now on.

He pulled out his cell phone and made the call.

## Chapter Eight

Oscar had just finished changing the locks and given her the new keys when her phone rang. She didn't recognize the number, but something told her to take the call anyway. "Hello?"

"Bella." She could barely hear her father's voice, but she immediately picked up on its urgency. "I've been arrested. I need you to get me a criminal lawyer. I'm so sorry." There was noise in the background. "I'm about to be booked on a drug charge. I got pulled over. They found drugs hidden in the door panel on the passenger side of my car. He put them there." His voice broke. "I have to go." The phone went dead.

She clutched her phone, closing her eyes and trying hard not to cry. Fitz. She'd childishly locked him out of the ranch house and this was how he was getting back at her. When they were kids, he'd been sneaky and vengeful. She knew better than to taunt him.

The new keys in her hand, she threw them across

the floor, angry with herself. If she was going to do something to him, then she had to be more careful. She had to be smarter. Taunting him would only make him tighten the screws on her father.

She had no idea how bad the drug charge would be—depended on how much was found in his car. While her father probably wouldn't get any time as long as it didn't appear he was selling the drugs, this would only add to the story Fitz was concocting against him.

Opening her eyes, she looked around the ranch. She and her father loved this place. She'd missed it desperately being away as she started her business. Now they were about to lose it. Her father was going to have legal fees, she thought as she made the call. Because of Fitz.

There had to be a way to stop the man before this ridiculous wedding. If she were stupid enough to marry him, he would find a way to take the ranch, she knew that, and her with it.

She spoke for a moment with a prominent criminal attorney a friend had used. As she hung up, she heard the sound of a vehicle pulling up. She took a deep breath. If it was Fitz, she feared what she might do that would only make things worse yet again. But it didn't sound like his sports car.

Bella stepped to the entryway, picked up the new keys from the floor and opened the door. Tommy Colt was climbing out of his pickup. Her heart leaped to her throat. He stopped to look up at her and she felt tears of relief fill her eyes. She'd never been so glad to see anyone in her life. He'd always been there for her—even after what she'd said to him on the street in town.

Propelled by nothing but raw emotions, she rushed down the steps and into his arms—just as she had in Denver.

THIS WAS NOT the reception Tommy had expected. Far from it. He breathed in the scent of her, the feel of her in his arms and held her tightly. She smelled wonderful, felt wonderful. He didn't want to let her go.

When she finally pulled back to look at him, he saw that she'd been crying. Again. "I'm in so much trouble, Tommy."

"I know. At least I suspect. That's why I'm here." He let her go as she stepped back and wiped her eyes.

"If Fitz catches you here—" Her voice broke. "There is so much I need to tell you. But not here." She seemed to be trying to come up with a place that was safe. Her green eyes widened. "Meet me at the tree house in ten minutes and I'll tell you everything."

He didn't want to leave her, seeing how upset she was, but quickly agreed.

"Take the back road out of here. Fitz can't see you," she said.

He could see how frightened she was and, while

he didn't like leaving her alone, he had to do as she asked. Clearly, she was afraid of the man. Tommy had never known her to be afraid of anything. What had Fitz done to put this much fear in her? He drove out the long way before circling back to the ranch's adjacent property—Colt Ranch property.

The road in wasn't as bad as the last time he'd seen it. They'd had a mobile home on the property to stay in when they were home from the rodeo circuit but one of James's girlfriends had rented it to some meth makers and had gotten it blown up. James had had the debris hauled off when he and Lorelei began building their house on another section of the property. Each brother had his own section to build on, if they ever decided to settle down.

Tommy parked and hurried through the pines toward the back side of Bella's ranch. He was scared for her, worried Fitz would come back and keep her from meeting him at the tree house.

But as he came through an open area, he saw her standing at the bottom of the ladder waiting for him.

The tree house looked as if it had weathered the years fairly well considering. "You'd better let me go up first," he said to her, seeing how nervous she was. He doubted her worry though was about the wooden structure the two of them had built together all those years ago.

One of the steps felt loose as he climbed up and pushed open the door. It looked as if some critters had made themselves at home in one corner, but other than that, the space looked better than he'd expected. He wondered if some area kids had discovered it and been keeping it up. There were several wooden crates someone had brought in. He dusted off one of them.

Turning he started to hold out a hand to help her up, but Bella was already coming through the door. He moved back to let her enter and handed her a crate to sit on.

For a moment they simply looked at each other, then she put down her crate and sat. He grabbed the other one, shook off the worst of the dust and sat down as well. The wooden crate creaked under his weight but held. He couldn't help but think of the hours he and Bella had spent here together, and the weekend they'd spent together recently. They had a bond that couldn't be broken, he told himself.

"A little different from that suite we shared in Denver," he said to break the silence. They'd watched movies, played cards, ordered room service and gone for long walks. They'd reconnected in a way that had made him realize that he no longer wanted to live without this woman by his side.

"So you're engaged?" he said even as he knew it couldn't have been her idea. He couldn't have been that wrong about her. Or how they both felt about each other.

Bella gave him a wan smile, tears sparkling in all that green before she dragged her gaze away. "I don't even know where to begin." He said nothing, waiting. "I told you that my father had called me and that I was headed home?"

From there she spilled out a story that shocked and infuriated him. "I'll kill the son of a—"

"No, that's just it. If either of us do anything, he'll just send my father to prison. He isn't bluffing. He planted drugs in my father's car and just had him arrested because I locked him out of the ranch house."

"You aren't seriously going to marry him," Tommy said, trying to tamp down his fury. He'd felt such relief when she'd told him that she'd been coerced into the engagement. But he hadn't realized how serious it was until now.

"I'm not marrying him," she said with a shake of her head. "But unless I can find evidence that proves my father is being framed..." She met his gaze. "I want to hire Colt Investigations."

He blinked. He had little PI experience. The skin around his eye was still bruised from taking Zeke in. "Bella, I appreciate your confidence in me but—"

"I'm so sorry for what I said on the street—"

"No, what I'm saying is that you need to hire an experienced investigator."

She shook her head. "You and your brother are the only people I can trust right now. I'll help. I know enough about my father's business and I have a key to his office—if Fitz hasn't had the locks changed. Will you help me?"

"You know I will," he said. He'd do anything for her. He realized sitting there, a shaft of sunlight coming through a slit between the old boards and lighting her face, that he would die trying to save her because he was crazy in love with her.

"But we can't be seen together," she said. "Fitz can't know that we've even talked after seeing us together in town. You probably shouldn't call me on my cell, either."

"I'll get us burner phones. I'll find us a safer place to meet." He grinned. "We grew up here. We know all kinds of places where we can be completely alone."

She smiled and let out a sigh. "I feel better than I have since my father called me. We can do this. We have to."

He nodded. "If you need to reach me before I can get the phones, call Lorelei and she'll get a message to me." He considered the trouble she was in and wished he could do more. Nothing like diving into a new job headfirst and blindfolded. But he was a fast learner and James would help from the sidelines.

She reached across the space between them and held out her pinkie finger. Tommy laughed at their old ritual they'd enact before leaving the tree house. He hooked his pinkie with hers.

"Best friends forever," she said and met his gaze.

*Till death do us part*, he thought.

## Chapter Nine

Bella hoped she hadn't made a mistake by dragging Tommy into this, but she needed help and he was the only one she trusted right now. She'd left the ranch house front door unlocked and was glad she had when she returned.

Fitz's sports car was parked in the drive. She circled around so it would appear she'd come from the trail along the river—rather from the woods that led to the Colt property.

"Where have you been?" Fitz demanded when she walked in the front door.

"For a walk along the river." She met his gaze. "My father's been arrested."

He nodded and smiled. "Drugs, huh. Such a shame. I see you left me a key to the house." His look said he hoped that she'd learned her lesson. He looked way too pleased.

But she had learned her lesson, she thought, heart pounding. It still took all her control not to attack him with her words let alone her bare hands. She warned herself to be smarter as she started past him toward the kitchen.

He grabbed her arm. She froze, telling herself to play along—but only so far. Glancing over at him, she gently pulled her arm free. "Unless you've hired new staff, I was just headed for the kitchen to see about dinner. I don't know about you, but I'm hungry."

He seemed surprised that she could cook. Let alone that she might cook for him. "What are we having?"

"I'll surprise you." Before she started away, she saw the wary look come into his expression and smiled to herself. Let him worry about her poisoning him.

In the kitchen, she turned her thoughts to Tommy Colt. She'd made the right decision telling him. He was her bestie. She'd realized how much he meant to her in Denver. The feelings had always been there, but she'd never acted on them. Neither had Tommy.

It was as if the two of them were giving each other space, knowing that one day… She shook her head at the thought. No wonder he'd been so upset to see the engagement ring on her finger. She couldn't bear that she'd hurt him. But everything had been happening so quickly.

Tommy. Just the thought of him made her heart ache. Once this was over… Right now she needed her best friend more than ever. Tommy was the only one she trusted with this news. With her life. He might be new to PI work, but he was smart and resourceful. Together, she had to believe that they could outsmart Fitz. They had to, because the clock was ticking. Fitz had already sent out the invitations to the wedding that was just over a week away.

BACK AT THE OFFICE, Tommy told his brother everything that Bella had told him. His gut reaction had been for the two of them to find Fitz and beat him senseless.

"Not an option," James agreed.

"But definitely what I want to do. Not that it would do any good. He's really set up Bella's father bad. We have to stop this before the wedding."

When he told him the wedding date, his brother groaned. "Nothing like a challenge. Are you sure about this? Bella is strong-willed as you already know. You sure she won't refuse to marry Fitz?"

Tommy shook his head. "She won't let her father go to prison. And neither of us think it's an idle threat. Fitz just had Nolan arrested in a drug bust. He planted the drugs. He did it because she locked him out of the ranch house. He's serious."

James shook his head. "He wants Bella that badly?"

Tommy looked away. "Maybe we should have been nicer to him when we were kids."

"Come on, I remember the kind of kid Fitz was. He's just grown up into a meaner adult. He sees

Bella as something he can't have so he's determined he will have her," his brother said. "She's probably the only person who's ever said no to him."

"So what do we do?" Tommy asked as he banked his anger.

"We need to get the proof. The truth will be in the real bookkeeping," James said. "Which means it's on a computer somewhere. Didn't the partnership have an accountant? I'd start with him." His brother thought a moment. "You've got to hand it to Fitz. He came up with the drug addiction as a way to show where the embezzled money went. Otherwise, there would need to be evidence of large expenditures like boats, cars, big vacations."

Tommy had a thought. "If you were her, wouldn't you demand to see the evidence he's holding over her head before she agreed to marry him?"

His brother beamed at him. "Very smart. That way we know where it is and how hard it will be to get. You think Bella will do it?"

He laughed. "We're talking about Bella, remember? She has more guts than anyone I know. But that doesn't mean that Fitz will go along with it."

As BELLA CAME in from the kitchen, she saw Fitz nervously rearranging the salt and pepper shakers, straightening the cloth napkins on the table and shifting his chair to put himself directly in front of the place setting in front of him.

She frowned as she put two plates of food on the

table, one in her spot and the other in front of Fitz. She realized this wasn't the first time she'd seen him do something like this. When he was a boy, he had to have everything just so from his clothing to his room.

As she started to sit down, he suddenly grabbed her plate and switched it with his. She looked over at him and smiled as she picked up her napkin and laid it carefully in her lap. "Have you ever seen the movie *The Princess Bride*?"

"Of course. It's…" Fitz frowned and then quickly switched the plates back, making her laugh. He looked miserable. Did he really want a lifetime of this?

Picking up her fork, she took a bite of her dinner. She'd had a lot of time to think while she was cooking. She would have to tread carefully. He'd proven today how vindictive he could be. Anything she did could have major repercussions for her father.

Bella looked up. Fitz hadn't touched his meal. "Is something wrong?"

He scowled at her. "I'm hiring a cook. You won't be allowed in the kitchen," he said angrily.

She shook her head. "Whatever you want, but I made that meal especially for you." She reached across the table, purposely knocking over the salt-shaker as she did, and jabbed her fork into a piece of the sweet-and-sour chicken dish she'd made.

Gaze locked with his, she brought the bite to her lips, opened her mouth and popped it in. As she began to chew it she watched Fitz pick up the salt-shaker and put it back exactly as he'd had it before. She reached over, this time just moving the salt-shaker a fraction of an inch out of line, and skewered a piece of pineapple.

She'd barely gotten the bite to her mouth when he grabbed the saltshaker, his hand trembling as he squeezed it in his big fist. She recalled how Fitz had always had to control things when he was a kid. Apparently, he hadn't changed—only gotten worse because now he thought he could control her.

"There is nothing wrong with the food on your plate," she said. "Cross my heart." She made an X over her heart and smiled.

Angrily, he shoved back his chair, knocking it over as he rose. "You like messing with me? Tormenting me? You should know better. Have you learned nothing today?"

"I haven't done anything but leave you an extra set of keys to *my* house and make you dinner." She reached over and stabbed one of the sliced carrots on his plate and popped it into her mouth. "You can't blame me if you're paranoid."

He was breathing hard, his face flushed. "I can't wait until we're married. I will make you pay dearly. Nolan always held you up as an example. 'Look at Bella. Isn't she amazing? So smart, so talented, so independent.'"

She looked into his eyes, feeling his hatred like a

slap. "Just because my father loves me and is proud of me—"

Fitz let out a bitter laugh. "He put you on a pedestal and stood next to you, just asking for someone to knock you both off."

"I'm sure he didn't mean to make you feel—"

"Like I could never measure up?" Fitz grabbed the chair up from the floor. For a moment, she thought he was going to hurl it at her. But he seemed to catch himself. He slowly lowered it to the floor and gently pushed it in. She could see him trying so hard not to reposition it perfectly.

"He was just proud of his daughter," she said again, quietly. But Fitz had seen it as her father comparing her to his partner's son. "With my mother gone—"

"Well, soon I will have his daughter and then we'll see how proud he is of you when he has to watch what I do to you."

Bella felt a shudder move through her. She had no doubt he would make good on all his threats. Now at least she had some idea why he was doing this.

"I'll be back with my things and a new staff, including a cook, first thing in the morning," he said. "I wouldn't suggest you do anything to stop me. Once we're married…" He sneered at her. "You will be mine to do with as I see fit in every way and there won't be anything you or your daddy can do about it." With that, he turned and left.

She felt a sob rise in her throat and tears sting her eyes. He planned to tear her down, dominate her, destroy, her and all to prove that he had always been smarter, more talented, more everything. He was fool enough to think it would make him feel better about himself.

Taking an angry swipe at her tears, she made a solemn oath that he wouldn't beat her down no matter how hard he tried. Nor would he destroy her because she was never marrying him.

She finished her meal, although she'd lost her appetite, but she wasn't going hungry because of Fitz. His hatred for her and her father scared her. She regretted involving Tommy and Colt Investigations. It terrified her, what Fitz would do if he found out.

Yet a part of her needed Tommy for support, needed his help. After their time in Denver, she'd missed him. Something had happened between them during that long weekend. Not that either of them had acted on it. But their feelings for each other had grown into something special that she hadn't anticipated. Or maybe she had, she thought with a laugh. Maybe that was why she'd looked up his rodeo schedule and made sure they'd crossed paths.

Given the way she felt about him, she told herself that once she got the burner phones he was picking up, she should fire him. This was her mess. She shouldn't have dragged him into it. Knowing how cruel and heartless Fitz could be, what would he do to Tommy if he got the chance?

She shuddered at the thought. But even as she thought it, she knew that Tommy would keep trying to help her even if she did fire him. The thought warmed her. The truth was she needed Tommy on so many levels. She couldn't do this without him. She'd just have to make sure that Fitz never knew.

When she finished dinner, she took their dishes to the kitchen. She was loading the dishwasher when she remembered something. About a year ago, she'd been home to the ranch and overheard her father on the phone arguing with Edwin. He'd been upset about some deal Edwin had made with a company called Mammoth Securities Inc. Her father had warned Edwin not to do it. She was pretty sure the man had gone ahead.

There might be something there she could use. With a sigh, she knew she'd have to ask Tommy to look into it. But with luck, they might be able to fight fire with fire.

She turned on the dishwasher and left the clean kitchen. She had no idea where Fitz had gone or when he would be back. She didn't trust anything he told her. She called Lorelei, James's fiancée. "Can you get a message to Tommy? Also, could you pass on a photo and some information I have for him?"

## Chapter Ten

Tommy had spent the day finding out everything he could about Edwin Fitzgerald Mattson the Third. Fitz looked good on paper, but the more he dug, the more questionable behavior he found.

He'd been reprimanded at boarding school for bullying. He'd also gotten into a cheating scandal at university. His father bought him out of both by making donations to the schools.

But Tommy had tracked down one of the former administrative assistants who'd been involved and gotten fired over it. The man had been most happy to give him the dirt on Fitz.

Unfortunately none of that would help the current situation, though. They already knew what kind of man Fitz was. What he discovered more recently was that Fitz had fired the partnership's long-time accountant six months ago. He felt that might be important since it was about the same time that Nolan Worthington had met the mysterious Caroline Lansing.

"How do we find this woman when we can't even be sure she gave Nolan Worthington her real name?" Tommy asked his brother.

James considered that for a moment. "Remember that kid in school, Lance Black's little brother?"

"Ian?" Tommy nodded.

"He's FBI. I think you should give him a call. Didn't you save his life that time in the river?"

Tommy laughed. "It wasn't quite that heroic. I did haul him out of the water, that much is true. But if you think he might help, I'll give him a call."

Ian sounded glad to hear from him. When he told him what he needed, Ian promised to see what he could find out. Tommy sent him the photo of Caroline and what information Nolan had given Bella and she'd sent to him through Lorelei.

"It's good to hear from you," the FBI agent said. "So you and your brother have taken over your father's PI business. Congrats. Probably safer than riding bucking horses."

Tommy wasn't so sure about that. "It's been interesting so far." He thanked him and then left to meet Bella.

He was already waiting for her at the abandoned old fire tower high on a mountain outside of town when she drove up. He could tell something more had happened even as she tried to hide it.

"You can talk to me," he said after they climbed up the four floors and took a seat on the landing. From here the view was incredible of the river valley and the mountains around them. They used to come here and drink beer with a friend who manned the tower during fire season. Now it was an empty locked shell that hadn't been used in years.

As the sun sank in the west leaving the sky blood orange, Bella nodded without looking at him and told him what Fitz had said to her. "I'm sorry I involved you. Fitz is dangerous. I can't let anything happen to you."

Tommy fought his anger, knowing, as James had said, if they did what they wanted to the bastard, it would only make things worse for all of them. He reached over and took her hand. "Nor can I let anything happen to you. I'm helping you no matter what you say. That's what we do, you and me."

She looked at him, those green eyes filling. "Tommy."

He put his arm around her and pulled her close. She felt warm and soft in his arms. He pulled back a little to look at her. All around them, darkness began to fill in under the towering trees. The air felt cool and crisp, scented with pine. The beautiful summer night filled him with memories of the two of them—and such love for this woman.

Tommy leaned closer, slowly dropping his mouth to hers. He brushed his lips over hers. He'd dreamed about kissing her from as far back as he could remember. He'd always feared that it could spoil their friendship. He was way past that now.

Her lips parted on a sigh as she leaned into

him. He pulled her closer, deepening the kiss. She wrapped arms around his neck and drew him down for an even deeper kiss. Their first kiss to the music of the summer night was everything he'd known it would be.

He drew back slowly and looked into her eyes. "The marriage isn't going to happen. We're not going to let it."

She nodded and snuggled against him as they looked out over the darkening land. After a while, he took one of the burner phones out of his jacket pocket and handed it to her. "Keep it close. My number is the only one in there."

She nodded and took the phone before telling him about the conversation she'd overheard between her father and Edwin Mattson.

"We're going to need to get into his office and Fitz's."

"I have the key to the main office door."

Tommy smiled over at her. "If Fitz is moving into the ranch tomorrow, I think we'd better break in tonight."

"I know the security guard should he stop by. He won't think anything about me being there. I just can't make things worse for my father. I got him a lawyer. He should get out on bail. At least for the moment. We discussed what he should do until his hearing and he's signing himself into rehab even though he doesn't have a drug problem."

"Smart. But I'm worried about you alone in that house with Fitz," Tommy said.

"There will be staff. I can hold him off until the wedding." She didn't have to mention that the wedding was coming up fast. He knew that Fitz had moved it up from the original date. The man certainly was in a hurry.

"There isn't going to be a wedding," he said again. "Let's go see what we're up against at the office. More than likely he wouldn't leave any evidence lying around. It's probably in a safe. Know a good safecracker?"

"No. I know a good locksmith, though," she said. "I also know Fitz." Then she leaned in and kissed him. "For luck," she said smiling.

THE OFFICE OF Lonesome River Investments was in the older part of Missoula on the river. The partnership had bought the narrow two-story brick building. It had a vintage clothing store on one side and a coffee shop on the other side, both leased to the businesses.

Bella used her key to open the outer door. They stepped into a stairwell and she locked the door behind him before they started up the stairs to the second-floor offices.

This floor had been completely remodeled with lots of glass and shiny metal. Her father, who'd originally started the business, had been content with the original exposed brick and worn hardwood floors. But Edwin had insisted appearance meant everything when dealing with other people's money.

She used her key to open the door off the landing and quickly put in the security code. She felt Tommy's worried gaze. Wouldn't the first thing Fitz would have done be to change the code?

No alarm sounded. Bella let out the breath she'd been holding, but grew more wary as she neared the separate offices. Edwin's was the first along the hall across from her father's. Fitz's office was behind his father's with storage and a conference room at the end of the short hallway.

She passed Edwin's dark office and headed straight for Fitz's. She told herself that while Edwin had to be in on this scheme, Fitz would keep the evidence close—not trusting anyone—including his father.

As she reached the door to his office, she was only a little surprised to find it locked. She and Tommy had expected this.

"I've got this," Tommy said and pulled out his lock pick set. "Thanks to my misspent youth." It took him only a few moments to get the door open.

"Nice job," she said. Both of them had gotten quite good at picking locks as teenagers. It was a skill though that they'd never imagined using at this age, she thought.

Once in his office, she turned on the overhead light knowing it would be less suspicious from the street to alert security. Her father paid for a security patrol in the area.

Bella went right to Fitz's desk. It was too clean. No desktop computer. No laptop, either. Which meant that Fitz always had it with him in that large briefcase he carried.

She wondered what he actually did for his pay here. She opened each drawer. All too neat. The bottom drawer was locked. She motioned to Tommy that she needed his lock pick when he was finished.

Tommy had gone to the filing cabinets against the wall, picked the lock and was now going through the files.

She was rusty at this, but the desk drawer lock was simple enough it didn't take her long. She opened the drawer. Empty except for a single folder. She pulled it out and placed it on the table. As she did, photos fell out and spread across the table.

Tommy was at her side in an instant, having heard the shocked sound she'd made. Every photo was of Bella. They appeared to have been taken over the years, most with a telephoto lens from some distance. Tommy was in many of the photos.

"What the hell?" he said as he went through them. "Sick bastard."

"He's apparently been spying on us for years," she said, surprised her voice sounded almost normal given the trembling inside her. She'd become the man's obsession long before she had any idea of what was going on in Fitz's mind.

"Has he been planning this for years?" Tommy said more to himself than her. He started to throw the photos in the empty trash can under the desk, but stopped himself. "This could be evidence if things go south." He pulled out his phone and spread the photos across the desk next to the calendar with "E. Fitzgerald III" on it and snapped a half dozen shots.

She put the photos back into the file and locked them in the drawer again. She felt uneasy and realized why. Had Fitz known she would break into his office? Had he put them in the locked drawer for her to find?

"Did you find anything?" she asked Tommy.

He shook his head as he started around the room, peering under the artwork until he found what he'd been looking for. Removing the painting that had been covering the safe, he took a photo of the safe. "You really do know a locksmith who might be able to open it?" he asked as she joined him.

"Maybe." Bella thought of the single file in the locked drawer. Fitz had known she would break into his office, break into his desk. She couldn't shake the feeling that he'd wanted her to find it.

She touched the dial on the safe and slowly began to turn it.

"Bella?" Tommy said next to her.

Not answering, she finished putting in her birthday. Something clunked inside the safe and the door popped open.

Tommy let out an oath. "What the—"

The safe was empty except for an envelope addressed to her. She hesitated before she pulled it out. It wasn't sealed. Taking out the folded sheet inside she read:

Did you really think I would leave anything here at the office, Bella? You think you know me so well, but the truth is I know you better. I've been watching you for years. That's why I can predict your every move. Speaking of moving, you should get out of there. The moment you opened the safe a silent alarm went off. Security will be all over this building within four minutes.

She crumpled the note in her fist even as she and Tommy quickly exited the building. They had planned to look around Edwin's office. Another time, she thought. Except next time, Fitz would have had the locks or the security code changed.

They were a block away when they heard the sirens and saw the lights as security descended on the Lonesome River Associates offices.

They would have already called Fitz.

FITZ SMILED TO himself as he hung up the phone. Bella thought she could outsmart him. He couldn't wait to see her face. But not tonight, he thought as he turned back toward the woman lying in bed. She was waiting for him, the covers pulled back, exposing her lovely breasts.

Bella was right. He could have most any woman he wanted, like this classic beauty waiting for him. He could do anything he wanted to her. That was what money and power got him.

Yet even as he had the thought, he felt his desire fade. There was only one woman he wanted. Bella. He told himself he would have her soon.

"You should go," he said, turning away to reach for his robe. "It's late."

"Are you sure?" She sounded disappointed even though he'd already had his fill of her.

For a moment, he reconsidered. A bird in the hand... Or in this case, a breast. He dropped his robe knowing this woman would do anything he asked her and come back for more.

"There's something I would like," he said and opened the drawer next to his bed. Her eyes widened and she drew back a little. "Is there a problem?" he asked as he pulled out the device.

She shook her head as he tossed her a gag and watched her put it on with trembling fingers. All he could think about was seeing that kind of fear and then pain in Bella's green eyes. She would learn soon enough who was in charge now.

"I HATE THE thought of you out at the ranch with that man," Tommy said when they reached the fire tower where they'd left his pickup earlier.

She'd turned off her engine, letting the summer darkness and quiet in. For a few moments, they sat in silence. "He thinks he knows me."

Tommy saw her shift her gaze to him in the darkness of the car. Overhead the sky was splattered with stars, but down here in the pines there were deep pockets of darkness.

"I'm afraid he proved tonight that he knows me better than I know him," she said, her voice breaking. "He's been one step ahead of me."

He reached for her, drawing her to him. She rested her head against his chest as he smoothed her hair. "He won't win. We won't let him. We can beat him, the two of us."

She nodded against his chest and pulled back, biting her lower lip for a moment. "What now?"

"James said you might want to demand to see what he's got against your father. That would let us know where he's keeping it. You could also demand an audit of the books. If Fitz wasn't expecting that move—"

"But if he is expecting it, that would alert the IRS of the embezzlement."

Tommy nodded. "It would mean calling Fitz's bluff. If the auditor suspected at all that there was a second set of books..."

She shook her head. "I don't know. So far Fitz seems to have thought of everything—the drugs in my father's car, the embezzlement, the setup at his office. Clearly, he's been planning this for a long time."

Tommy nodded. "It's a risk, but it could buy us time."

"Let me think about it," Bella said. "Maybe I'll talk to my father. I don't know that Fitz showed him the doctored books. You could be right and they don't even exist."

Tommy nodded and said, "Exactly," but he thought she was probably right the first time. Fitz had planned this. There would be doctored books. What if an audit only put her father in even more jeopardy with the law?

"What did you find out about Mammoth Securities Inc.?" she asked.

"Edwin dumped it at a loss," Tommy said. "That's all I've been able to find out."

Bella started the car. "I'll call you tomorrow the first chance I get."

He wanted to warn her to be careful. But she knew better than anyone what was at stake—and how dangerous Fitz was. "I did want to ask you to marry me." The words just came out as he reached for his door handle and looked back at her.

She smiled. "Is that right?"

Tommy nodded. "I still plan to." With that he got out and headed for his pickup. Had he looked back he would have seen her smiling.

## Chapter Eleven

Bella had seen the vehicles pull up in the ranch yard last night from her bedroom window. As she watched a half dozen men exit the vehicles, Fitz drove up and got out of his car before leading the men into the house. Even from where she stood watching, she could see that the men were armed. Several of them looked like thugs. She noticed that those two were the ones Fitz had pulled aside to talk to.

Fitz was preparing for war, she thought, imagining the ranch becoming a fortress to keep only one person in—her. After that, she'd had a fitful night, sleeping little. This morning she'd showered and dressed, determined not to let Fitz get to her.

Her cell phone rang and she saw it was Whitney. She hadn't spoken to her since they'd gotten together after her weekend with Tommy. "Hey," she said as she picked up.

"What is going on? I just heard that you're

engaged to Fitz and getting married in a matter of days?"

"It's a long story. I can't get into it right now," she said, wondering if one of the guards was listening outside her bedroom door. "Needless to say, things have been a bit complicated since I returned to the ranch."

"What happened with Tommy?" her friend asked, sounding sad.

"I still feel the same and I'm pretty sure so does he. It's going to work out." Her voice broke. "It has to." She hoped she sounded more positive than she felt right now. "Think good thoughts for me."

"You know I will. I'm a hopeless romantic."

She disconnected and started down the hallway to the stairs. As she did, she heard Fitz's raised voice coming from the guest quarters. Glancing around, she checked first to make sure none of his security was around before she moved down the hallway. Stopping at his door, she listened. He was angry with someone. She didn't catch a lot of his words. He seemed to be walking around with the phone.

"I don't care what you think," Fitz snapped. "I want this and damned if I won't have her."

Bella felt a chill as she realized that he was arguing with someone about her.

"You will back me on this or I'll take you down with him," Fitz yelled. "That's right, you don't think I didn't see this coming?" The laugh made her shudder. "That's right, you did teach me everything I know. Thanks, Dad. But if you bail on me now you'll wish you hadn't."

At the sound of footfalls coming up the stairs, she hurried down the hall before she turned and pretended to only just now be leaving her room. Her heart pounded so hard she thought for sure the security guard who appeared would be able to hear it.

She gave him a smile, but he barely gave her a glance, confirming what she'd suspected. They'd been told not to interact with her in any way. Of course Fitz would want them only loyal to him. The rough-looking guard continued on down the hallway toward Fitz's room. She heard him knock and Fitz open the door and call him by name. Roman. Fitz asked about Milo.

Roman said Milo was on his way. Then the door closed and she could no longer hear their voices. She swallowed, straightened her spine and went downstairs, but had barely reached the first floor when she heard someone coming. The men he'd called Ronan and Milo exited the house without a word.

Right behind them was Fitz. He saw her and he gave her that annoying smirk. It had changed little from the time he was a boy. But now she saw satisfaction in his eyes. They were dark, brooding, so different from Tommy's sky blue eyes that spoke of summer days and sunshine.

"Have a nice night?" Fitz asked as if he'd secretly

put spiders in her bed. She could imagine what he'd been like at camp—if he'd ever gone.

"Actually," she said, thinking of Tommy's last words to her, "I did." She smiled, turning his smirk into a frown. "I see you *bought* some friends."

He started to correct her when he realized she'd purposely not said *brought*. She watched him grind his teeth for a moment. "I want you to be safe so I've hired some men to make sure you are."

They had lined up in the living room as if waiting for assignments. Bella knew it was Fitz's idea, a show of force. None of them scared her as much as Fitz himself.

"One of them is a cook?" she inquired. "I hope so because I haven't had my breakfast yet." She knew that needling Fitz wasn't smart, but she couldn't stand how self-righteous he'd looked when he'd entered her house last night with his soldiers as if it were his own. It would be soon enough if he got his way, she reminded herself.

"Roberto," Fitz snapped. "You're in charge of the kitchen. I don't want Bella to lift a finger in there. In fact, I don't want her in there at all. Can you make sure she has no reason to enter?"

"Yes, sir," Roberto said and looked toward her. "Just tell me what you would like for breakfast, Miss Worthington."

The man showing her respect clearly grated on Fitz. She could see him struggling to keep from saying something.

"It's Bella and thank you, Roberto. Surprise me."

As if he could take no more, Fitz barked orders to the five other men to act as security for the ranch house and her. She realized he must be putting them up in the bunkhouse, which meant they would be on the property 24/7 until the wedding.

Bella took a seat at the table in the dining room to wait for her breakfast even though the thought of food made her sick to her stomach. But she would eat every bite even as her stomach roiled. It was clear what Fitz was doing. How long before he ordered the men not to let her leave the house?

Roberto made her huevos rancheros. When she told him that she loved Mexican dishes, he promised to order chorizo, pinto beans, all kinds of peppers and tortillas to make some dishes she might like.

She thanked him and ate her breakfast, which was delicious and seemed to calm her. Her thoughts ricocheted back and forth from dark ones of Fitz to happier ones of Tommy. When she finished, she knew better than to take her plate to the kitchen. She unhooked her shoulder bag from the back of her chair and headed for the front door.

Her burner cell phone was hidden in her car. She'd felt it would be safer there than in her purse or even in her room. Fitz had already shown how low he would stoop. She knew it wouldn't be long before he started going through her things.

She had just reached the front door when she heard Fitz behind her.

"Wait!" he called, his footsteps heavy on the stone floor. Her skin crawled as he came up behind her. "Where do you think you're going?"

She took a deep breath and let it out slowly before she turned to face him. "I'm going into town to get my hair trimmed and my nails done. Do you have a problem with that?"

"I don't think it's safe, you running around with that big rock on your finger," Fitz said. "I'd prefer you take one of our security guards with you."

"I'd prefer not." She pulled the ring from her finger and dropped it unceremoniously on the entry table. It rattled as it skittered across the glossy top, coming to a stop on the edge before almost plummeting to the stone floor. "Problem solved," she said and reached for the door handle.

He grabbed her arm and jerked her back around to face him, squeezing her wrist until she let out a cry. "Haven't you caused enough trouble for your poor father? You don't want to underestimate how far I will go. You will do as I say."

"So you think," she spat over the pain as he continued to grip her wrist nearly to the point of breaking it. "But you will keep your hands to yourself and I will do as I please. You take it out on my father again and I will slit your throat while you sleep. Try me, if you don't believe me."

Fitz let go of her, flinging her arm away. "Once we're married—"

She didn't wait to hear the rest of his declaration

as she held back tears of pain, turned and walked out the door. She figured he would station a security guard at his door tonight—and probably one at hers as well.

Tommy had been expecting Bella's call. "Hey," he answered, relieved. Every moment she was in that house with Fitz she was in danger. "You all right?"

"Fine."

He heard too much in that one word. "What's happened?"

"Just Fitz being Fitz," she said, brushing it off. "I'm on my way to Edwin Mattson's office. I heard Fitz arguing with him on the phone this morning. He might help us."

"I'll meet you outside of town at Four Corners. We can leave your car there," Tommy said and disconnected. Four Corners was an old café and gas station where two county roads crossed.

On the drive into Missoula, he broached the subject. "Maybe you should move off the ranch."

"Even if I would give him the satisfaction, he wouldn't allow it. He's made it clear that he'll do even worse to my father. Last night he moved a half dozen security guards onto the ranch. Earlier…" She seemed to hesitate and he saw her touch her wrist. "He tried to keep me from leaving."

"If he hurt you—"

"I told him that until the wedding, he wasn't to touch me and that I would do as I pleased."

"And he agreed to that?"

"*Agreed* probably isn't the right word, but he didn't try to stop me." She turned to look at him as he drove. "Don't worry about me. I can hold my own."

He didn't doubt that under normal circumstances. But this was Fitz. And now he had security guards at the ranch?

"We just need to get our hands on whatever he tricked my father into signing. Maybe Edwin will help us."

Tommy had his doubts, but he didn't voice them. Edwin and Fitz had always seemed a lot alike, two peas in a pod. But if Bella was right and Edwin was against this, then maybe he would help. Unless he was just as scared of what his son was capable of doing as the rest of them.

"Did you know that six months ago, your father and Edwin's company changed tax accountants?" She shook her head. "I suspect it was Fitz's doing. He didn't want their old accountant to catch any red flags."

"So six months," she said. "That at least narrows it down."

He nodded. "Which means past tax returns won't help until we have the current records. I'm wondering if it would do any good to talk to the former, fired accountant."

Bella smiled over at him. "I knew coming to you was the right thing to do."

Tommy took her hand and squeezed it, hoping

she didn't regret it. "But first we see Edwin. Fitz already knows that you broke into the office. I don't think it hurts for him to know that you're not alone in this, that I'm doing everything I can to help you."

She nodded but he could tell she was worried. "Just be careful."

"I will. I don't think he'll do anything more to your father at this point," Tommy said, hoping that was true and glad when she agreed.

There was no one at the front desk when they entered the main office. He saw Bella glance at the empty assistant's desk and frown. The nameplate on the desk read Dorothy Brennan, he noticed as they passed.

They walked down the same short hallway they had the other night. Edwin's door was slightly ajar. Bella pushed it open.

The white-haired man behind the desk looked up. Tommy hadn't seen Edwin Mattson in quite a few years and was shocked by how much he'd aged. He seemed surprised to see them. Not just surprised, but nervous.

"What are you…" He looked at the landline phone on his desk as if wanting to call someone for help. Dorothy? Or Fitz?

Tommy closed the door behind them and locked it.

Edwin's eyes widened. He stumbled to his feet. "Bella, what… If this is about Fitz… None of this is my doing. You have to understand—"

"I do understand," Bella said as she stepped into the room and took a chair. Tommy continued to stand, his back to the door. "I heard you on the phone this morning with Fitz. He's got something on you as well as my father."

Edwin slowly lowered himself back into his chair. "I don't know what to say."

"I thought you and my father were friends," she said. "You really won't help him?"

The older man wagged his head. "I can't, even if…"

"What is Fitz holding over your head?" she asked. "Mammoth Securities?"

His eyes widened. "How did you know about—"

"I overheard my father telling you not to get involved with them."

Edwin looked sick. "I should have listened to him."

"Which is also why you can't let my father go to prison for something he didn't do. Fitz has no conscience but I'm hoping you do."

The older man reddened as he looked up at her. "It isn't like your father is completely innocent. He's embezzled money from the partnership before."

"That's not true," she snapped.

"I'm afraid it is. That time, I caught it and we remedied the problem before it was discovered. I would imagine though that it is where Fitz got the idea to use it against Nolan."

Tommy could see that Bella was shaken. "When

was this?" she asked and listened as Edwin gave her the details. "But this time?" she asked, her voice breaking.

Edwin shook his head. "I don't know. Fitz swears Nolan's at it again. Are you aware that he has a drug problem?"

"Fitz or my father? My father definitely doesn't. It's all part of this web of lies that Fitz is spinning to control me. That's why I need to prove that Fitz is trying to frame him," Bella said.

"It isn't that easy," the older man said with a sigh.

"Why is that?" Tommy asked.

Edwin seemed to recognize him then. "You're one of those Colt boys."

"Tommy Colt. I'm working with my brother at Colt Investigations."

The man nodded, looking sicker, as if things had gotten even worse. "You realize that if Fitz finds out you came to me…" Edwin shook his head. "You'd be wise not to cross him. Either of you. You have no idea how far he'll go."

"Oh, I have a pretty good idea," Bella said. "Surely you can see that he'll take you and my father down as well. He can't be trusted to keep his word—even if I did marry him."

"If you don't marry him…" Edwin looked terrified at the thought of what his son would do. "I wish I could help, but my hands are tied. You coming here with…" He glanced toward Tommy again.

"You're only making matters worse for yourself. Once Fitz has made his point—"

"You don't believe that. He's determined to destroy me and my father. It sounds like he plans to do the same to you."

Edwin started to come around his desk. "I'll see you out."

Tommy shook his head as he unlocked the door. "Don't bother. You made this monster. You need to take care of it."

"Tommy's right," Bella said. "You're just as guilty as he is if you don't do something to stop your son."

"Don't you think I would have stopped him a long time ago, if I could?" Edwin demanded and followed them to the door to slam it behind the two of them.

As they were leaving, Bella slowed at Dorothy's desk and picked up what appeared to be a dead potted plant before heading for the door.

"Are you all right?" he asked once they were outside. She was hugging the pot with the dead plant, looking close to tears. "Edwin could have been lying." He didn't believe that and he knew she didn't, either, but she looked as if she needed a little hope. He glanced at the pot. "I hate to even ask."

"Dorothy. Her plant is dead." Bella met his gaze. "Which means she not only got fired, but also left in a hurry without her plant."

"Sounds like Fitz is cleaning house," Tommy

said. "First the accountant, now the administrative assistant. You thinking what I am?"

Bella glanced at her cell phone. "I want to talk to her, but I can't be gone any longer today. I'm hoping to get into Fitz's room when he leaves again."

"Please be careful," Tommy said.

"Believe me, I am," she said. "How are you doing on tracking down the company's former accountant?"

"Working on it." He hated to tell her that the man seemed to have disappeared.

## Chapter Twelve

Fitz was waiting for her when she entered the ranch house. "Roberto has made us a special dinner."

"I'm not hungry," she said.

"Please join me. I have something we need to discuss," he said. "Unless you no longer care what happens to your father." He started to take hold of her arm, but then seemed to think better of it even though clearly she wasn't really being given a choice about dinner.

"Why don't you lead the way," he said and stepped to the side to let her pass. "We're having steak, my favorite. As I recall, you don't like steak. Probably because you had so much of it growing up. There was always beef in your freezer, wasn't there."

"I was raised in Montana on a cattle ranch," she said as she stepped past him. Even though they hadn't touched, she still felt her skin crawl. But what Edwin had told her about her father's earlier embezzlement had her shaken. If true, could it also be the case this time as well?

"Yes, growing up on this ranch," Fitz said. "That's probably why you didn't appreciate it and why you looked down your nose at me when I always asked for steak when we visited here."

"Stop pretending you were some poor kid who went without food. If I looked down my nose at you, Fitz, it was because you were as rude, obnoxious and demanding as a boy as you are now as a man," she said as they entered the dining room, where Roberto was ready to pour the wine. "I see you've gotten into our wine cellar as well as into our freezer," she said under her breath.

Fitz seemed to clamp his jaw down as he took his chair and Roberto helped her with hers. The wine poured, Roberto went into the kitchen, leaving them alone. Bella watched Fitz straighten everything before settling back in his chair. She could imagine what life would be like married to this awful, self-absorbed man. She felt sorry for any woman innocent enough to marry him. It certainly wasn't going to be her.

"Did you have a nice day?" she asked as she took a sip of her wine. He wanted to play at being husband and wife? She'd play along—to an extent.

"Very much so," he said. "And you?"

"It could have been better," she said and put down her wineglass after taking a sip. It was one of her father's expensive wines, which came as no surprise. Of course Fitz would help himself to the best. But she had to keep her wits about her.

Out of the corner of her eye, she noticed that the door to her father's den was open. But it was what she saw inside that made her momentarily freeze. Her father's gun safe stood open. There were no guns inside.

She looked at Fitz, who was smiling. She smiled back. Was he so afraid that she might shoot him? Was he going to hide all the knives in the kitchen as well? She would have found it amusing under other circumstances, she thought, as Roberto brought out their meals.

"Your father made bail, I heard," Fitz said. "I suppose you've talked to him. I hope he's doing all right. Maybe we should have him committed to rehab—at least until the wedding. What do you think?"

She met his gaze and laughed. "Actually, he committed himself. He needs a good rest and it will look good when he has to go before the judge."

Fitz's surprise that he'd been outmaneuvered was wonderful to see. She took pleasure in it, wanting to gloat. She and her father had anticipated what Fitz would do next and had beaten him to the punch.

He picked up his knife and fork and began to hack at his steak with angry jabs at the meat. "You didn't get your hair trimmed or your nails done."

She said nothing. He wanted her to know that he'd checked up on her. That he would be check-

ing every time she left the house—if not having her
followed. She'd never been fond of steak but sliced
a bite off and put it in her mouth.

Moments before, she'd been gloating—a mistake.
If she thought she could beat this man at his game,
she'd better think again. She chewed and met his
gaze head-on. "No, I didn't go. I changed my mind.
I was too upset after I left the house."

"So what did you do?" he asked as he took too
much time cutting his steak. He knew she'd posted
her father's bail. She should have seen it in his
smugness the moment she saw him before he'd insisted she join him for dinner. But he'd gone straight
to rehab.

"I'm curious," she said, not answering his question. "Is your plan to marry a woman who you're
determined to make hate you to the point that she
would kill you in your sleep?"

He looked up from his steak. "Do you really
think I care how you feel about me?" He laughed.
"This won't be a real marriage, Bella. Once I completely destroy you and your father, once you're
flat broke and broken, I'll dump you in the street.
I'll sell your precious ranch and I'll move to some
exotic place where I can have any woman I want—
just as you said."

His words shocked her more than they should
have. Wasn't this exactly what she'd thought he
would do? He'd never wanted her. This was about
humiliation. He'd felt small around her and her fa-

ther. Apparently he couldn't live with that unless he brought her down and her father with her. Which meant even if she agreed to marry him, he would still send her father to prison.

"You do realize how pathetic that makes you sound, don't you?" she asked and took a bite of the twice-baked potato on her plate.

Fitz bristled, slamming down his knife and fork. Both clattered to his plate. A piece of steak flew off and onto the tablecloth. "I know you went to see Edwin. You and Tommy Colt. Did you really think my father wouldn't tell me?"

Bella considered that for a moment. She'd seen how scared Edwin had been of his only son. She should have known he'd tell Fitz, fearing that Fitz would find out and punish him even further.

She could see that Fitz was having trouble leaving the bite of steak on the tablecloth. Grease had started to leave a stain. She leaned forward, warning herself that she was taking this too far, but unable to stop herself. She snatched up the piece of steak from the table and tossed it back on his plate.

"You know what I think?" she said at his horrified look. His gaze kept going from the stain on the tablecloth to the piece of steak balancing on the edge of his plate. "I think this has something to do with your mother leaving you when you were five." All the color drained from Fitz's face. "I heard your father tell mine that you cried for days. I can't imagine how traumatic that must have been for you. I think it explains a lot about why you're acting out now and why—"

Fitz shot to his feet, overturning his water glass and knocking his chair backward. It crashed to the floor. "If you ever mention my mother again—" The words spewed from his mouth along with spittle.

"I'm just trying to understand where all this hate comes from," she said. From the look in his eyes, she'd taken it too far and yet it didn't feel like far enough at all. Look what the bastard was doing to her family.

For a moment, she thought he might have a heart attack. He stood swaying slightly as if trying to speak, but no more words came out. He heaved, each breath labored, his eyes poison-tipped darts aimed straight for her. When he did start to move, she realized he might launch himself across the table and go for her throat.

She picked up her knife. *Let him come.*

"Mr. Mattson? Can I get you anything else? Dessert is almost…" Roberto realized he had interrupted something. "Ready."

It took a moment for both of them to acknowledge that they were no longer alone. Fitz seemed to take a breath, his gaze shifting from her to the table and finally to Roberto standing in the kitchen doorway.

"Clean up this mess," Fitz snapped and shoved away from the table to storm out of the room.

Bella slowly put down her knife. "I think we're finished, but thank you, Roberto." She hated to think what might have happened if the man hadn't interrupted them.

"I will see that some dessert is sent up to your room, Miss—Bella," Roberto said.

She smiled at him as she put down her napkin and rose. "Thank you." She almost warned him that being kind to her would get him fired. But her heart was still in her throat. How would she survive this? Unless she could find a way out, she wouldn't.

## Chapter Thirteen

To Bella's surprise there wasn't a guard outside her door the next morning. She'd had a fitful night filled with nightmares. As she made her way down to breakfast, she wasn't looking forward to seeing Fitz after last night. She told herself she would try to be pleasant. Even as she thought it, she found herself grinding her teeth.

But as she approached the dining room, she heard the sound of his sports car engine rev. When she looked out, she saw him speeding away.

Was he going into Missoula to see his father? She wondered if she should call Edwin to warn him. Then again, Edwin had told Fitz about their visit and had refused to help, so she figured he was on his own. After all, Fitz was his son.

"Good morning," Roberto said as he came into the dining room. "I have a special breakfast for you. Please have a seat."

She felt as if she were in a fancy restaurant rather than at the ranch. Her father had a cook who made meals when they were here at the ranch and had company. The rest of the time, they did for themselves.

"I have for you this morning quesadilla frita," Roberto said with obvious pride. "Two crispy tortillas topped with black beans, layered with fried egg, ham and cheese, and topped with my special spicy sauce. Served with a side of fried plantain."

"This looks wonderful," she said, admiring the dish. She asked about this family and if he'd always enjoyed cooking.

"I would spend time with my grandmother in Mexico," he said. "We would cook together. Everyone loved her cooking. I hope you enjoy your breakfast," he said and retreated to the kitchen.

Bella dug in, surprised by how hungry she was before she realized that she hadn't eaten but a couple of bites of dinner last night. After she finished, she stuck her head into the kitchen doorway and thanked him.

Then she'd hurriedly gotten ready to leave before Fitz returned. Her first stop was the rehab center her father had checked himself into. It was small and expensive and more like a spa than rehab, but money well spent if it helped should this ever go before a judge.

She found her father sitting out in the garden. He heard her approach, his expression brightening at the sight of her. She joined him on the bench and let herself breathe. Her father looked good, although she could still see fear in his eyes.

"I can't stand the thought of you having to deal with Fitz alone," he said, glancing around to make sure no one was listening. They were alone in the garden except for a man trimming a hedge in the distance. The buzz of his saw sounded like a swarm of bees.

Bella turned her face up to the warm sun. She took a deep breath and caught the scent of freshly mown lawn and pine from the nearby trees.

"I'm not alone," she said. "I've hired Colt Investigations."

"You aren't serious?"

She turned to meet his gaze. "I trust them. They are about the only ones I trust right now. You didn't tell me that this isn't the first time money has gone missing. Only last time, you paid it back."

"Who told you that?" her father demanded.

"Edwin."

Nolan Worthington slumped a little on the bench and turned his face away. "I'd made a couple of bad investments. You were in college. I couldn't borrow any money from the bank without worrying clients… So I borrowed some from the business."

Bella shook her head. "Is there more I don't know about?"

"No," he said, turning back to her. "I swear. But that's probably what gave Fitz the idea. It was stupid, but fortunately Edwin caught it and I sold some assets over time and paid every cent back."

"How do I know that this time is any different?" she asked.

His face reddened. "I didn't take the money." Her father shifted on the bench. "But no one is going to believe me if my own daughter doesn't."

She said nothing for a few moments as she tried to breathe. The sky overhead was cornflower blue, dotted with cumulous clouds that morphed in the breeze. She loved Montana summers. They always reminded her of Tommy. Back when they were kids the summer seemed to stretch out before them with so many possibilities.

Now she could feel the days slipping past, headed for the train wreck of a wedding that she wasn't even sure would save her father if she was stupid enough to let Fitz force her into it.

Her father spoke, drawing her out of her thoughts. "About six months ago, I was considering retiring. I'd had enough of Fitz. Edwin was cowed by him. I wanted out of the partnership, but Fitz wasn't having it. He made me an offer for the ranch." Her father hurried on as he saw her horrified expression. "I told him he'd never have the ranch, that I had my lawyers put it in your name. He got really upset."

She stared at him. "You think that's when he decided to force me to marry him for the ranch?"

Nolan shrugged. "I doubt it's that simple. Fitz probably doesn't even know what he wants. It's just something he doesn't have. Maybe he thinks if he had you and the ranch, he would be happy."

She laughed. "Is he really that juvenile? I would make his life a living hell and enjoy every minute of it." Bella couldn't believe this. The ranch was safe as long as she didn't marry Fitz—if she did, under Montana law he would own half of it. But she thought her father was right. It wasn't the ranch Fitz wanted so badly. He wanted revenge for feeling less around her and her father and the ranch.

Nolan reached over and took her hand. "I got myself into this mess. You need to let me get myself out even if it means going to prison."

She sighed. "You know I won't let that happen."

"I'm not sure either of us has a choice," he said, letting go of her hand. "But if you marry him—"

"Don't worry," she said, getting to her feet. "I'm not going to marry him. I'll find a way out of this for both of us."

Her father still looked as scared and worried as she felt. She touched his shoulder. "I'll think of something."

As she left, Tommy called.

"I got an address for Dorothy Brennan, but we need to hurry," he said. "Her landlord said she gave notice and is in the process of moving out." He rattled off the address. "I'll meet you there."

DOROTHY BRENNAN HAD been with her father's company from as far back at Bella could remember. A tall, thin, serious woman, she'd kept small treats in her desk for when Bella visited her father at work.

The one thing she knew about Dorothy was that she loved plants. The one on her desk had been started from a cutting her grandmother had given her.

While she'd never married or had children, Dorothy had kept this plant alive for decades. That was why when Bella had seen it sitting on the woman's desk dead, she'd known something was terribly wrong. Dorothy wouldn't have left that plant behind.

Tommy was parked down the block when Bella arrived. She parked and got out as he joined her. They walked up the driveway to where Dorothy was loading boxes into the back of her SUV.

When she saw Bella, she started and glanced around as if expecting…who? Edwin? Fitz? Or the cops? The woman looked haggard and scared. Her gaze lit on the pot Bella was carrying and hope shone in her eyes.

"Miss Brennan," Bella said, calling her by the name she always had, as she approached. Tommy quickly took the box from the older woman and put it into the SUV for her. "This is Tommy Colt, a friend of mine. Could we talk to you for a moment?" She held out the pot. "I'm sorry about your plant, but I couldn't leave it in that office."

Dorothy took the pot, looked down at the skeleton of her dead plant and hugged the pot to her. For a moment she studied each of them, then nodded and led the way inside the apartment. There wasn't much left except a couch and chair and a bed in the one bedroom that had been stripped. Bella assumed someone would be picking up the larger, heavier items and taking them wherever the woman was headed.

"Please sit down," Dorothy said as she set the pot on a windowsill in the sun. "I'd offer you something to drink but..." She glanced around, her throat working.

"We don't need anything but a few minutes of your time," Bella said quickly. "What happened at the office?"

The woman's gaze was shiny with tears as she turned to her. "I was fired. In a text from the young Mr. Mattson. I tried to go back for my things, but I was met at the door by two security guards and told I couldn't enter. I asked for my plant and was told it had been thrown out."

"I'm sorry," Bella said, touching the woman's shoulder. "This was Fitz's doing?"

Dorothy shrugged. "He's the one who gave me notice, but I assumed the others knew."

"My father wasn't involved," she said. "He's been pushed out as well."

She saw concern in the woman's face. "Nolan was always kind to me. I'm sorry."

"You aren't surprised that my father was forced out."

Dorothy shook her head. "I knew something was going on."

"Do you know what?" Bella asked.

"I heard things about Nolan, but I didn't believe them."

"Fitz is blackmailing my father, saying that Nolan embezzled a lot of money. He says he has proof."

"We suspect he has doctored books that show the losses coming from Nolan," Tommy said.

"There was money missing," Dorothy confirmed. "I heard Fitz arguing with his father about it. Edwin said that if it got out to clients it would destroy the business."

"If my father didn't take the money..."

The older woman met her gaze. "It was Fitz. You've seen his sports car?" Bella nodded. "It's just the tip of the iceberg." For a moment, Dorothy didn't look as if she was going to continue. "There's the country club and his lunches with so-called clients. But his big expense is his gambling and the woman he's putting up in a penthouse in Spokane."

"Do you have the woman's name and address?" Tommy asked.

Again Dorothy hesitated but only for a moment. "I wrote it all down. I was angry. Not that I thought I could do anything about it." She went to the few items she had stacked by the door, picked up her purse and opened it.

From inside, she took out what appeared to be copies of expense sheets. "These are the real ones," she said, handing them to Bella. "These are the ones he turned in to the business. I've been keeping two sets and keeping my mouth shut. He told me that if I talked, he'd say I stole from the company and have me arrested. He made me sign a nondisclosure agreement in order to get my last paycheck."

"Don't worry, I'll make sure it never comes back on you," Bella said, knowing that this wasn't enough to stop Fitz anyway. But it was a start. "Do you have any idea where he's hiding the evidence that would show my father took the money?"

Dorothy shook her head. "I'm sorry. Clearly he didn't trust me." Her voice broke. "But…" She hesitated, then Bella saw the woman make up her mind. "One time I walked into his office and startled him. He quickly pulled a thumb drive from his laptop and palmed it until I left. I think that is probably what you're looking for."

Bella looked around the almost empty apartment. "Where will you go?"

"To Florida. My sister's until I can find another job."

"Send me your address. I'll let you know how it all ends." If it ended the way she hoped, she would get Dorothy a decent severance package from the partnership or die trying.

"I hope Fitz gets what's coming to him," Dorothy said.

"So do we," Bella agreed. Her cell phone rang. She checked. "Speak of the devil," she said. "I have to answer this." She stepped outside. Behind her, she heard Tommy asking if he could help Dorothy load anything else.

"Hello."

"Where are you?" Fitz asked. When she didn't answer, he said, "I'm making wedding plans. I need to know what your favorite flowers are."

Tommy joined her. Having overheard, he nodded and mouthed, "Tell him baby white roses."

She frowned since things were never going to go this far. Nor were those her favorite flowers and Tommy knew that. "Baby white roses."

"Excellent. That was going to be my choice," Fitz said, sounding relieved that she wasn't fighting him.

"Lonesome Florist," Tommy mouthed. His friend owned it, but she couldn't see why that would make a difference.

"I like the ones they have at Lonesome Florist," she said. "Since you're asking."

Fitz chuckled. "Got it. Oh, and you have a dress fitting scheduled tomorrow at two."

Bella looked at Tommy and had to bite down on her lip for a moment. "How thoughtful. You didn't trust me to select my own wedding dress?"

"I think you'll find that I have excellent taste," Fitz said with his usual arrogance. "I might surprise you." She shook her head but said nothing. "I'll leave the information about your fitting on the entry table in the hallway since you're spending so little time here."

"Is that all?" she asked.

"I heard you went to see your father," Fitz said. "I hope he's doing well."

"I'm sure you do," she said sarcastically. "Good-bye." She disconnected.

"He thinks your father is why you're not being so difficult," Tommy said. "So let him think that."

"Let him think I'm giving in to him?" she demanded as she pocketed her phone and shook her head. "He'd be more suspicious if I played nice, trust me. What was that about the flowers and the shop?"

"Just covering our bets. The owner is a friend. If it gets down to the wire, I could get you a message hidden in baby white roses."

Her pulse rate soared at the thought of it going that far. "Now what?"

"It seems like it wouldn't be that hard to prove that Fitz lives beyond his means and that he's the one who's been embezzling the money," Tommy said. "Have you thought any more about asking him for evidence?"

Bella shook her head. "Don't forget he's already framed my father for drug possession. But I might ask him before the fitting tomorrow to show me the proof of my father's embezzlement."

"At least Nolan's safe where he is now. I think we should check out Fitz's woman in Spokane. It will take all day to go there and come back. Sounds like you're busy tomorrow."

She hated it, but nodded. "I think I'd better go to the fitting. I can only push him so far without it hurting my father."

## Chapter Fourteen

Bella was relieved to see Fitz's car gone when she returned to the ranch. Several of the guards though could be seen on the property. She ignored them and hurried inside.

Roberto had made her a special dinner, but she didn't do it justice. She kept thinking about Tommy and their first kiss and smiling stupidly. She'd known it was inevitable and that once they stepped across that line there would be no going back. The kiss had been just as wonderful and magical as she knew it would be.

Sitting on the deck of the fire tower had been the perfect spot to finally kiss. The summer night, the closeness she and Tommy had always shared, the chemistry that had always been there all added to that moment. But now she felt herself aching to be back in his arms. She wanted more. But also she knew how careful they had to be. If Fitz found out…

She heard his car engine. A few minutes later he walked in carrying his briefcase and frowning. She wondered what he did all day. It hadn't crossed her mind until that moment that maybe things weren't going so well for him—and that it might not have anything to do with her. She thought about what Dorothy had told her. Was it possible her father wasn't the only one who was broke? If Fitz was hurting for money, then he needed what he could get for the ranch. Which meant he had to get her to the altar post haste.

The thought gave her little comfort as he came into the dining room. Roberto must have heard him. "Can I get you some dinner?" he asked Fitz, who shook his head and waved him away.

The cook quickly slipped back into the kitchen, letting the swinging door close behind him. She wondered if Roberto stood on the other side listening. Not if he was smart.

"Did you already eat?" she asked pointedly.

He met her gaze, still standing over the table holding his briefcase. "No, I'm just not hungry, but I see you've had your fill."

Food shaming? It made her smile. "And I enjoyed every bite."

That wasn't what he'd wanted to hear. "Some of us have to work. How is your business doing without you?"

"Who says it's without me?" she said, even though she hadn't given it much thought since her father's call. Fortunately, she'd hired good help and they were keeping things going without her.

"I wonder what you do all day," he said, narrowing his eyes at her.

"I wonder what you do all day," she said, narrowing her eyes at him.

He shook his head. "I'm not up to sparring with you tonight." He turned his back on her and started to walk away.

"I want to see proof that my father was embezzling money from the partnership," she said before he could escape.

He stopped but didn't turn around. "Why now?"

"I was remiss in not asking sooner."

"You wouldn't be able to understand it all. But an auditor would, especially one from the IRS." His threat hung in the air.

"I'm a lot smarter than you think. I run my own business," she reminded him. "I'm going to need to see it or the engagement is off."

He turned then. The look in his eye made her shudder inside. She realized she could have chosen the wrong time to make any demands.

She watched him fighting to keep his temper in check, refusing to drag her gaze away first or move a muscle.

"Tomorrow. After your wedding dress fitting," he said, his voice hoarse with emotion. "I'm too tired tonight." With that, he turned and stalked off, his spine rigid with anger.

She watched him storm up the stairs and disappear before she let out the breath she'd been holding.

TOMMY KNOCKED ON the penthouse door. He'd brought a box of chocolates and a bouquet of flowers. He'd thought he'd have trouble getting past the security guard at the desk.

"Mr. Mattson was very specific. I am to take these to her door and make sure she gets them," he told the desk guard who started to argue. "He wants me to make sure she is alone," Tommy whispered. "If I don't call back soon…"

"Fine, but be quick. I'll call up to let her know you're coming."

Tommy stopped him with a look.

"Fine. Just go up. She's in number two. The passcode is 409." He waved him away as if to say that both the woman upstairs and Fitz were a pain in his behind. Tommy didn't doubt it.

The elevator let him out on the top floor. He walked down the hall to number two and knocked, wondering what kind of reception he would get. He couldn't wait to see what kind of woman Fitz would actually pay money to keep.

He made a mental bet with himself. The door opened. He lost the bet. Worse, for a moment, he was speechless. "Margo Collins?"

"Yes?" The resemblance to Bella was shocking. Long dark hair. Green eyes. On closer inspection, he could see that she looked nothing like her beyond the obvious. Bella's features were softer and she was a little shorter and curvier.

"I have a delivery," he managed to say around his shock.

"From Fitz?" Margo asked and frowned. "He never gives me flowers but especially not chocolates. He says they'll make me fat."

"I guess he changed his mind," Tommy said, seeing that he'd messed up already.

"Well, it's okay with me," she said with a giggle as she outstretched her arms for her gifts.

"Mr. Mattson also wanted me to pick up something for him while I'm here."

She studied him for a moment as if noticing him for the first time, then shrugged and said, "Come in."

He followed her inside the apartment. Everything was white from the walls to the ceiling to the carpet on the floor and the furnishings. There were large windows that looked out on the hillside and the city.

Margo headed for the kitchen with her presents. In the living room, the television was on a reality show. The place was so clean and neat, Tommy couldn't believe anyone actually lived here.

He noticed her rummaging around in the bouquet and realized that she was looking for a card from Fitz. "Mr. Mattson said he didn't need a card because you already know how he feels about you." Her face lit up. "I need a folder he thinks he left here."

"In here?" she asked and turned toward what appeared to be an office.

Margo busied herself, humming as she put her flowers into a vase and opened the box of chocolates.

"Oh, Fitzy, you really are going to make me fat. You never give me candy. Are you being a bad boy?" She chuckled as she popped a chocolate into her mouth.

In the small office, Tommy quickly checked the desk. None of the drawers were locked. Nothing in them hardly. Nothing of interest, either.

He looked up. Margo was standing in the doorway holding her box of chocolates. "You must be a new one," she said. "Didn't find what you were looking for?"

He shook his head. "He said there were some papers…"

"I bet he put them in his briefcase and forgot he took them," she said with a chuckle. "That thing is practically attached to his arm lately, but I guess I don't have to tell you that. Kind of like that thumb drive around his neck. I asked him what was so important. He said it holds the key to his heart." She smiled and licked her lips. The scent of milk chocolate wafted toward him. "You won't tell him I said that. He says I need to say less and think more." She shrugged. "He's right." She looked sad for a moment, then considered her next piece of chocolate from the box and brightened.

"Don't worry, I won't mention it if you don't mention that I didn't find what he sent me for. Like you said, the papers are probably in his briefcase and he forgot. I don't want to tell him that he messed up."

She nodded knowingly. "Smart. Our secret."

"Maybe the flowers and chocolates should be,

too. I have to confess. They were my idea. I thought it would be rude to just show up without something." He gave her his best sheepish look.

She looked guiltily down at the box in her hand. She'd already made a good dent in the contents. He watched her debating what to do.

"Probably best not to mention the chocolates especially," she said.

He nodded and smiled. She seemed nice enough, though naive. "Our secret. Want me to bring anything else if he sends me back?"

She nodded with a laugh. "Surprise me. And stop by anytime." As he started to leave, she added, "If he does remember why he sent you here, could you remind him about the rent? The landlord called again." She made a face. "When Fitz gets busy, he forgets stuff. But it's been a few months now."

Tommy nodded, feeling sorry for the woman. It appeared Fitz was phasing her out as he got closer to getting what he really wanted. Tommy wondered how to tell Bella what he'd found out. It gave him a chill as he recalled how much Margo had looked like her—at least at first glance and when she smiled.

The memory sent a sharp blade of fear through him. Apparently Fitz wanted more than revenge for what he saw as her ignoring him all these years. He wanted Bella.

## Chapter Fifteen

The next morning, Fitz was already gone by the time Bella came downstairs. She'd lain awake wondering how Tommy's trip to Spokane had gone. She didn't dare get her phone from where it was hidden in her car to call him. She'd pushed Fitz about as far as she thought she should for one day so hadn't left the ranch the rest of the evening.

Roberto had made her another delicious breakfast. She ate it quickly and, grabbing the note Fitz had left her with instructions to her dress fitting, she left. Once out of sight of the ranch and the guards, she called Tommy.

They met at a spot on the river north of town. As she parked in the pines and followed the sound of the water to the river, she thought about all the times she and Tommy had come here. They used to love where the stream pooled in the rocks to make a deep swimming hole.

Tommy sat on one of the rocks near the pool. She hopped from rock to rock to drop down beside him. The rock under her felt warm in the sun. She closed her eyes and leaned her head back to enjoy the rays for a few moments, before opening her eyes and looking over at him.

The news wasn't good. It showed in his handsome face. Those Colt brothers, she thought as she smiled to herself. They were a handsome bunch. "What don't you want to tell me?" she finally asked as she found a small piece of rock and threw it into the pool. She watched it sink until it was out of sight before she looked over at him again.

He hadn't shaved, his designer stubble making her want to kiss him. She couldn't help herself. She reached out, cupped that strong jaw and drew him to her. The kiss was sweet—at first, almost tentative. She touched the tip of her tongue to his and felt him shiver before drawing back.

"You keep doing that and you know where this is headed," he said, his voice rough with emotion.

"Would that be so bad?" she whispered.

He brushed his fingertips lightly over her cheek. She closed her eyes as his callused thumb caressed her lower lip. She wanted him with every fiber of her being. Her body tingled at his touch. She wanted to lie in the nearby grass naked in his arms.

Opening her eyes, she met his gaze. His desire mirrored her own, but there was also regret there.

"Bella." She heard the pain in that one word. "All this isn't dangerous enough for you?"

She felt the impact of his words. Not for her,

for her father. If Fitz knew, he would hurt her father. She leaned back, needing to put a little distance between them. Her pulse thrummed. Only moments ago, she was ready to suggest they go into the woods. This had been building between them for years and she wanted it more than her next breath.

Closing her eyes against the desire that burned inside her, she let the sun again warm her face. "You haven't told me about Spokane." She realized that whatever he'd found out yesterday, it hadn't just made him more cautious. It had made him scared. For her father? Or for her?

"So what's she like?" she asked without opening her eyes. The sun felt so good, the smell of the river and the pines so crisp and familiar, she could almost pretend that none of this was happening. Just another summer day in Montana, her and Tommy on the river.

Tommy was quiet for a moment. "Margo Collins is like you."

She looked over at him.

"She looks so much like you that when you first see her it's startling," he said. "But then you see the differences, until she smiles. She has your hair, your eyes, your smile. Or damned close. As close as Fitz could find."

Bella let out a ragged breath. A sliver of disgust at the perversity of it followed on the next breath by fear that worked its way under her skin to her veins before roaring through her. The woman more than resembled her? She wasn't sure what she'd been expecting. Just some woman Fitz was keeping, but she should have known it was more than that. He'd kept this woman secret. He didn't want anyone to know. Maybe especially Bella. "Did she tell you anything we could use?"

He shook his head. "She isn't involved in any way in his business from what I can tell. She's just…an ornament. Until he gets the real thing."

TOMMY WALKED BELLA to her car. "Call me later." He could tell that she was as shaken as he was by what he'd discovered. Now at least she understood. They both did. A man who just wanted to destroy didn't go to all this trouble. Fitz wanted Bella. The woman Tommy loved.

But for how long? Fitz had no idea what he was wishing for. A woman like Bella would never be dominated by a man or anyone. But it seemed Fitz wanted to try—and would do anything for the chance.

"I told Fitz I wanted proof of my father's crime. He was in a really weird mood last night and said he'd show me after my dress fitting today."

"How weird?" he asked.

"Like he'd had a bad day at the office. I don't think it was because of anything we did unless…" She met his gaze. "You don't think the girlfriend called him and told him about you stopping by?"

Tommy shook his head. "I don't think so. Maybe all this isn't going together as well as he'd hoped. I'll see what I can find out. I think I might have located the former accountant. I'm meeting with him later. If he shows up. He sounds scared."

She nodded, but he could see that she was distracted. He wanted to hold her, to kiss her and get back that moment by the river. But it was gone and any intimacy seemed like a very bad idea until they got her and her father out of this mess. Fitz was too dangerous. And not just to Nolan. Tommy worried what the man might do to Bella—the two of them basically alone in that house with Fitz believing he could do anything he wanted.

"I'll call you later," she promised. "Tommy?" He had started to walk away but turned back. "Be careful."

He smiled. "You, too."

"Yes, I wouldn't want to get stuck with a pin at my dress fitting." With that she started the SUV and drove away. He watched her go before heading to his own rig. He was anxious to talk to the partnership's former accountant. As he reached his pickup, he heard a vehicle engine start up in the distance and realized they might not have been alone.

THE BRIDAL SHOP was in Missoula so Bella had way too much time to think about everything that Tommy had told her on the drive. She felt as if Fitz had a life-sized doll of her hidden in Spokane. It gave her the creeps. Worse, it seemed Tommy was right. Fitz wanted the real thing—her.

He'd said this marriage was in name only, but she suspected he would never let her go once he got her legally bound to him. He wanted her, the ranch, everything he felt he'd been cheated out of in life. So basically, he had no idea what he wanted to fill the cavernous yearning hole in him.

She found the bridal shop, parked and climbed out of her SUV. As she did, she saw a black pickup pull in a couple of vehicles behind her. She recognized the man behind the wheel and felt her heart drop. It was one of the guards Fitz had hired.

Heart in her throat, she realized he could have followed her from the ranch this morning to the river. He would know that she met Tommy there. She felt herself flush, remembering the kiss and the embrace. Only a fool wouldn't have realized how intimate it had been.

She was thankful that they hadn't taken it further on the sunny shore under the pines. Fitz was dangerously close to following through with his threats. For her sake and her father's, she needed to be sure that he didn't snap.

Taking a few breaths, she tried to assure herself that if she had been followed, it had only been from Lonesome to Missoula. She watched him get out of his pickup. He didn't look in her direction as he walked into a boot shop, letting the door close behind him.

Was it possible she hadn't been followed at all? It could be the man's day off. He could have just happened to be in the area. She wished she could believe that as she entered the bridal shop. The bell over the door tinkled and a young woman appeared.

"Bella Worthington?"

All she could do was nod, her mouth was so dry.

"Why don't you come back? I have your dress ready. I'm Crystal."

Her legs felt like jelly as she walked toward the back. Before she stepped through a curtained doorway, she glanced back. She didn't see the guard from the pickup. She pushed through the curtain and tried to still her raging heart.

Tommy was right. They had to be more careful. Which meant they couldn't chance being together. The thought hurt her physically. She ached to lie in his arms, to feel his body against her own, to feel safe and loved and fulfilled.

"Step in here," Crystal said. "You can hang your clothes there while I get your dress. Did you bring shoes?" Bella hadn't. "It's all right. Your fiancé said you probably wouldn't. He thought of everything." The young woman turned and walked away. Fitz had thought of everything. Wasn't that her greatest fear?

She had a sudden urge to call Tommy on the burner phone and warn him to be careful. If she was right and the guard had followed them to the river, then he might have already given that information to Fitz.

But the burner phone was in the car. She reached for her purse, thinking it wouldn't make a difference now if she called Tommy on her cell. Not if Fitz already knew that she and Tommy had been meeting secretly. Had the guard seen them kissing? Had he taken photos from a distance?

Fear for Tommy's safety had her fumbling in her purse when Crystal returned holding the wedding dress. Bella froze. Not because of the dress. But because of the man standing behind Crystal.

"Fitz?" Her voice sounded too high to her ears. "What are you doing here?" Her mind was working. Whirling. She grasped the only thing she could think of. "It's bad luck to see the bride in her dress before the wedding."

"Don't worry," he said, his expression souring at her response to seeing him. Crystal had noticed and was trying not to show it. "I was just dropping off your heels that go with the dress."

Bella swallowed. "Thank you. That's very thoughtful. You know how stressful this is for me."

His frown softened. "I know. But now you can relax. Crystal, I think my fiancée is going to need that glass of champagne we talked about before she tries on her dress."

Crystal snapped right to it, hanging the dress on a hook in the large plush dressing room and scurrying out.

Fitz stepped in. "I was thinking about this time when we were kids. I sprained my ankle and you got a bag of frozen peas for me to put on it. Which proves you can be nice to me."

She lowered her voice so Crystal didn't hear. "My father is the one who made me be nice to you when we were kids. Yes, the same one you're trying to put in prison."

"Not if you marry me."

She gave him a side eye. "That would require trusting you."

He seemed surprised. "What would it take? Actually…" He held up his hand to stop her from answering. "People have been wondering why we don't go out together. So I was thinking…dinner tonight at the steakhouse? Don't say no."

She started to tell him that it would take more than a dinner at the steakhouse, but he didn't give her a chance. No doubt he already knew what she was going to say.

"Please don't tell me you're too busy to have dinner with your fiancé." His smile never reached his eyes. "You have been awfully busy lately. Maybe if you had your friends to the ranch instead of meeting them elsewhere…at least until the wedding…" She heard what he was telling her loud and clear. He knew about her and Tommy. Did he know it had gone beyond just friendship? Did he also suspect that she'd hired Colt Investigations to help her? She figured he would find that more amazing than worrisome. He didn't think much of her intellect or Tommy's, she was sure.

"I appreciate your concern," she said, hoping he didn't hear the break in her voice."

"Of course I'm concerned," he said, looking as if he thought he had everything under control. "Soon we will be husband and wife. Then I'm going to take care of you." It sounded like the threat it was.

Crystal reappeared with her glass of champagne. Bella took it with trembling fingers as Fitz excused himself to take a call. She couldn't hear what was being said. Her heart was pounding too loudly in her ears. Tommy was in trouble. She could feel it.

"Great," Fitz said after finishing a quick call. "A romantic dinner tonight at the steakhouse. It's just what we both need." He stepped close again, leaning toward her. She jerked her head to the side and his kiss brushed her cheek. "I'll see you later," he said as his cell phone began to ring again.

"You are so lucky to have such an attentive fiancé," Crystal said as Fitz disappeared from view.

Bella saw the questioning look on the young woman's face. Downing the champagne, she handed back the empty glass, making Crystal's eyes widen. "You have no idea."

She could hear Fitz's voice on the phone. It sounded as if he were pleading with someone. The sound faded as the bell over the front door tinkled and he left. "I need to make a quick call," she told Crystal and dug out her phone.

"I'll get your veil," the young woman said and left with the empty champagne glass.

Bella called Tommy's cell, but it went straight to voice mail. The back of the shop was quiet. She was pretty sure that Fitz had left, but she never knew for sure, did she.

"He knows," she said into Tommy's voice mail. "Be careful, please." She disconnected as Crystal returned.

"Ready?" the young woman asked.

Bella nodded. She wondered how many nervous brides came through here and how many of them were having second thoughts. She doubted there were many like her, trying on a wedding dress she'd never seen before in heels she hadn't purchased with only one thought in mind: killing her fiancé rather than going through with the wedding.

FITZ LEFT THE dress shop congratulating himself on not losing his temper with Bella. When he'd gotten the call from Ronan earlier today, it had confirmed what he'd feared. Bella had been meeting Tommy Colt—just as she had when they were kids. Only Ronan had seen the two locked in an embrace that he'd described as "hot."

His first instinct was to throw her father to the wolves and then go after her. But he'd reminded himself that he had the upper hand only with the threat of sending her father to prison. If he hoped to get her to the altar, then he had to leave Nolan alone.

As for Bella herself... He'd wanted to grab her by the throat, and shove her against the wall in the bridal shop and... He shook his head. Fortunately, he'd kept his temper. She would be his soon enough. In the meantime, he had to deal with everything else going on.

He needed money. A few investments that didn't pay off like he'd hoped, the expense of this wedding and all that entailed and some bad luck. The past few times he'd gotten into a high-stakes game, he'd lost. Worse, he had some loans coming due—not to mention all the payments for his expensive lifestyle.

As he was driving out of Missoula, he saw a Realtor sign and swung into the parking lot. It was a little premature, looking into selling Bella's ranch. But once they were married, he had plans that didn't include keeping the place. He had a general idea of what all that land along the river might be worth. Add the house, stables and barn, it should more than take care of his problems.

Fitz told himself that everything was going to work out and when it did, he would have Bella. But first he had to make sure that Tommy Colt didn't go near her again. He pulled out his phone and made the call to Ronan, who was still tailing the Colt PI.

By the time he came out of the Realtor's office, he was humming "Wedding March." Things were looking up.

THE BAR WHERE Tommy was meeting the accountant was small and dark and on the wrong side of the tracks in Butte. Because of the hour, there were only a few patrons inside at a table and a couple at the bar. The only person by himself was a man sitting at the far end of the bar away from the couple.

Tommy took a stool next to him. "Bill McMillan?"

The fiftysomething man was dressed in a suit, his tie loosened at his neck. He smelled of men's cologne and sweat, his dark hair flecked with gray and slicked down with something shiny.

"I'm sorry I said I'd talk to you," the man said.

The bartender wandered down. Tommy ordered a beer and looked to Bill. He sighed and nodded as if resigned to getting drunk. He already had two empty drink glasses in front of him.

Tommy waited until their drinks came. He took a sip of his beer before he spoke. Next to him Bill took a gulp of his drink. He started to pull out a pack of cigarettes before apparently remembering that he couldn't smoke in a bar in Montana anymore. Swearing, he gripped his glass with both hands and stared into the dark amber contents.

"Why do you think Fitz fired you?" Tommy asked after a moment.

Bill glanced over at him. "For obvious reasons." He lowered his voice although no one was paying them any attention. "He was robbing the company blind, and I was tired of covering for him."

Tommy took a wild guess. "He wouldn't cut you in."

The accountant looked offended and for a moment, he feared Bill would get up and walk out. "I was going out on a limb for this jackass. It was the least he could do to make it more worth my while."

"How'd you hide it from his partners?" Tommy asked and took another drink of his beer without looking at the man.

"I set up a shell company for him. I'd write checks for fictitious expenses. I'd cash the checks and he'd take the money."

"Is there any way to prove he was involved?"

Bill leaned an elbow on the bar to look at him. "That's the really stupid thing on my part. I made it where he could walk away clean. It would look like I was taking the money because his delicate little hands never touched a pen."

"Wouldn't all of this show up on bank records or corporate business filings with the state?" Tommy asked.

"They could. Why do you think I left without a fight? He has me right where he wants me. He wouldn't give me a recommendation. I'm having hell finding another job. He could send me to prison. I'm the one who was writing checks and cashing them," Bill said.

"What about his bank records?"

The man shook his head. "Fitz wasn't putting the

money in the bank. There was no paper trail back to him—only me."

"So you cooked the books, hiding the money that Fitz was stealing from the partnership until he fired you and got a new accountant," Tommy said, trying to understand how this all worked. "Is the new accountant involved?"

"Hell, no. Right before he fired me, he shut down the operation by killing off the shell company, making it look as if he sold the businesses at a loss. The problem is, now there is no extra money coming in. The only money he has is from the partnership with his old man and Nolan Worthington. I'd say with his gambling problem and his flashy lifestyle, he's in need of a cash infusion."

Tommy thought about the marriage to Bella. He had no idea what she might be worth. Her business was too new to be making much. But the ranch was in her name. Was that what Fitz was after besides Bella?

Bill drained his drink and slammed down his glass. The bartender headed in their direction. "One more for the road."

The bartender hesitated.

"I can give him a ride," Tommy said. As soon as the bartender left to make that drink, he asked, "Isn't there a record somewhere that proves there was a shell company but no real businesses?"

"Sure, if you knew what you were looking for." Bill shook his head. "That's how these guys get away with it. They kept their hands clean and let someone else take the blame. Fitz didn't set up the shell company. He had one of the partners do it."

Nolan? Or his father? Tommy couldn't help his surprise. "Wait, you're saying one of the partners was in on it with him?" Bill shrugged. The bartender returned with his drink and looked at him pointedly. "I'm giving him a ride." He turned to Bill the moment the bartender was out of earshot. "Which partner?"

Bill took a gulp of the drink. His eyes were half-closed now. He seemed to be having trouble staying on the stool. He loosened his tie some more and shook his head. "Nolan, but he didn't know what he was signing. He'd made a couple of bad investments and was running scared. He signed whatever I put in front of him."

Downing his drink, Bill half fell off his stool.

"Come on," Tommy said. "I'll drive you home."

"I didn't drive," Bill slurred. "I walked. I live just down the alley. I can find my way home blind drunk, trust me."

"Well, I'll see you home anyway," Tommy said as the man staggered toward the back door. Throwing some money on the bar, he hurried after him.

Pushing open the door, he stepped out to see that Bill was already partway down the alley. Tommy had just started after him when he heard an engine rev and tires squeal. He looked down the alley to his right and saw a dark-colored vehicle headed directly for him.

## Chapter Sixteen

Bella still hadn't heard from Tommy by the time her fitting was over. She headed back to the ranch, half hoping Fitz wouldn't be there. But of course he was there waiting for her, sitting outside in the shade of the porch.

"How did it go?" he asked as she climbed the steps.

"Fine." She headed for the door.

"You didn't say anything about the dress."

She stopped, her hand on the doorknob. "It's a nice dress."

He laughed. "That's the best you can do?"

Bella turned to look at him. "What do you expect, Fitz? You know I don't want to marry you and that none of this would be happening if you weren't blackmailing my father."

"I wish it hadn't come to this, either," he said. "But you've never given me a chance."

She sighed. "I don't feel that way about you. It's simple chemistry. I can't control it." She saw his expression harden and reminded herself that they weren't capable of having an honest conversation without him getting angry.

"But there's chemistry between you and that saddle tramp Tommy Colt?" he snapped. He seemed to instantly regret his words as he hurriedly got to his feet and moved toward her. "Bella, I'm sorry. Let's just go to dinner and not discuss anything but the weather. Montana in the summer. We can agree on how wonderful it is, can't we?"

She realized that she feared this conciliatory Fitz more than the angry one. It made her worry all the more about Tommy. She couldn't wait to get to her room and try his cell again. It was dangerous using her regular cell phone to call him. But maybe it made no difference—if as she suspected Fitz already knew about the two of them.

"I'll go change for dinner," she said and entered the house, leaving him on the porch. She hurried up the stairs to her room, locking the door behind her. In the bathroom she turned on the shower in case someone was listening outside her door. She made the call, but like before, Tommy's cell went straight to voice mail.

TOMMY YELLED FOR Bill to watch out and threw himself against the bar's back door he'd only closed moments before.

The vehicle blew past him, hitting several garbage cans lined up along the edge of the building.

Tommy ducked as one of the cans careened into him, knocking the air out of him. Out of the corner of his eye, he saw the front of the vehicle strike Bill, tossing him into the air. As the vehicle sped away, Bill's body landed in a stack of cardboard boxes piled behind a business. The accountant crumpled to the ground and didn't move.

Hand shaking, Tommy pulled out his phone as he ran toward Bill and punched in 911. Crouching next to the man, he checked for a pulse, shocked that Bill was still alive as the 911 operator answered.

He'd stayed with Bill until the ambulance arrived along with the first cop. Tommy had turned off his phone to talk to the police about the hit-and-run. He was still shaken. "It happened too fast. No, I didn't get a license number or see the driver. All I can tell you was that it was a black SUV."

Another cop arrived at the scene and pulled him aside. This one was older with buzzed gray hair and pale intense eyes. "You say the driver swerved toward you first, then ran down Mr. McMillan?"

"It appeared that way, yes. Look, like I said, it happened so fast. I was getting ready to go after Bill to make sure he got home. The SUV must have been parked down the alley waiting. I hadn't noticed it until I heard the roar of the engine and the sound of the tires squealing."

"Is there anyone who might want to kill you?" He could feel the cop's gaze intent on him.

"Not that I know of," Tommy told him. Fitz hated

him and had proved how low he would stoop to get what he wanted. But murder?

"I recognize your name. Rodeo cowboy, right?"

"Was," Tommy said. "I recently joined my brother at Colt Investigations."

The cop's expression changed. "So this could be about some case you're working on."

Tommy hesitated, not sure what to say. "I really doubt it."

"Let me be the judge of that," the cop said. "Who's your client?"

"That's confidential."

The officer stared at him. "Seriously? Someone tries to kill you and you prefer not to tell me who you're working for?"

"Like I said, I doubt it's connected."

With a disgusted sound, the cop put his notebook and pen away. "Have it your way."

"How is Bill?" Tommy asked.

"Last I heard he has a broken hip but was in stable condition. You said he was extremely intoxicated?" Tommy nodded. "Being inebriated probably saved his life."

The cop got a call on his radio. All Tommy heard was "stolen black SUV." When the cop finished he looked at him and shook his head. "Could have been some teen joyriders. Guess we'll know more when we find the vehicle."

With that the cop walked back to his patrol car and Tommy turned on his phone and saw that Bella had called numerous times. He quickly dialed her number as he headed for the hospital.

BELLA AND FITZ were about to be seated at the steakhouse when her cell phone buzzed in her purse. She started to reach for it when Fitz's hand clamped over hers.

"Not tonight," he said, his hand tightening on hers.

"Just let me turn it off." He glared at her for a few moments before his grip loosened.

She quickly dug out the phone. Just as she'd hoped, the call had been from Tommy. She turned off her phone seeing that he'd left a message she would check later as they were escorted to their table.

The moment she saw where they would be seated, Bella knew this was Fitz's doing. It was in a back corner, secluded. A candle flickered on the table and a bottle of champagne chilled in a bucket of ice next to two glasses.

Fitz pulled out her chair for her before going around to his. She could tell that he was determined to be pleasant—as hard as it seemed for him sometimes.

"Are we celebrating something?" she asked, relieved that she'd heard from Tommy—otherwise she would have worried given how in high spirits Fitz seemed tonight.

"Our first real date," he said and gave her a look

that dared her to argue otherwise. He poured her a glass and handed it to her before pouring one for himself and offering a toast. "To the future. May it be happy for us both."

She wasn't sure how that would be possible, but she clinked her glass against his and took a sip. The bubbles tickled her tongue. She tried to relax, telling herself that Tommy was fine. He had gone to talk to the accountant. Maybe it had taken longer than he'd thought it would, but if he'd found out something they could use…

"You look so beautiful," Fitz said.

"Thank you." She picked up her menu. She wasn't hungry, but she was determined to get through this so-called date.

"I know you're not much of a steak eater," she heard him say. "But they have seafood. I know you like lobster. Please, this is my treat."

She lowered her menu. "Is everything all right?"

"Why would you ask that?" he inquired, frowning.

"It's just that you're being so…"

"Nice?" He let out a chuckle. "Did you really not realize how I felt about you all these years?"

She shook her head and dropped her voice even though there was enough noise in the busy restaurant that she doubted anyone could hear. "I thought this wasn't going to be a real marriage. That you were just doing this to destroy me *and* my father."

Fitz reddened and dropped his gaze. "I was angry

when I said those things. I wanted to hurt you because you've hurt me." He raised his eyes to hers again. She saw him swallow before he spoke. "That wasn't what I really wanted. I've been in love with you for years."

After what Tommy had found out in Spokane it didn't come as a complete surprise. "You just have an odd way of going about asking me out."

He took a sip of his champagne before settling his gaze on her again. "You would have laughed in my face, but let's not get into that now. I want us to have a pleasant dinner. Is that possible?" Bella nodded, not up to one of their usual battles, either. "Have the lobster. I'm having a shrimp cocktail before a steak entrée. Join me. I know how much you like shrimp."

The waiter appeared and she nodded as Fitz ordered for them. Anyone watching might have thought that they were really engaged and having a nice quiet dinner before their upcoming wedding.

Bella tried to relax, but not even the champagne helped. This whole thing was a farce and worse, she sensed there was something Fitz wasn't telling her. He was in too good a mood. She felt as if she was waiting for the other shoe to drop and when it did, she knew it was going to be bad.

The rest of the evening was uneventful enough as they both steered away from anything resembling the truth.

It wasn't until they were leaving the restaurant

that two men came out of the shadowy darkness of the parking lot and accosted Fitz.

"Here," he said to her, shoving his keys at her. "Go on to the car and let me handle this." She took the keys but didn't move. The men were large and burly and clearly angry. "Go!" Fitz snapped and gave her a push.

She stumbled toward the car. When she looked back, Fitz was arguing with the men. One of them shoved him back into the side of the building. Clearly they were threatening him. She couldn't hear exactly what was being said, but she'd picked up enough of it to know it had to do with money and gambling.

At the car, she opened the door and climbed in. Fitz appeared a few minutes later. He looked shaken. "What was that about?"

"Nothing," he snapped. "Drop it, okay? Just a misunderstanding. Everything is fine."

Bella really had her doubts about that. However, she could tell by the change in Fitz's mood that unless she wanted trouble from him tonight, she needed to let it go. But she couldn't help but wonder if Fitz was in financial trouble. If he owed those two men from the parking lot, then he had more than money problems.

Maybe this wedding wasn't just all about her after all. She had a bad feeling that her ranch had even more to do with it.

## Chapter Seventeen

Bella woke with a start. For a moment, she didn't know what had yanked her out of her deep, mentally exhausted sleep. Her cell phone rang. She blinked, still fighting the coma-like state she'd been in only moments ago, as she reached for it and realized it was early morning. She'd tried to call Tommy last night but with no success. His message on her phone had been short: *I'm fine. Will call later when I can*.

She checked the screen and saw that the call was coming from Lonesome River Investments, her father's office. "Hello?" She sat up, thinking it couldn't be her father. He was still in rehab. Or was he? "Hello?" She could hear someone breathing on the line. "Dad?"

"It's Edwin," said the male voice. Fitz's father. The man sounded drunk.

"Are you all right?" she asked and heard him chuckle as she leaned against the headboard. This felt like the extension of the dream she'd been having. She wasn't sure any of it was real. "Edwin?" She heard him clear his voice.

His words were slurred when he finally spoke. "I... I thought about what you said." She held her breath. "You're right. Fitz won't stop. Even when he was little we noticed something was... That he was a challenge." He sounded as if he was struggling for his next breath. "But he's my son." He broke down for a moment.

"I'm so sorry. I know how hard this must be for you."

The man seemed to pull himself together. "You can't marry him."

"I don't plan to. Give me something to stop him."

For a moment she thought he'd disconnected. "He has a thumb drive on a chain around his neck. He did that after he caught me checking his deposit box at the bank."

She realized that she'd seen Fitz toying with the gold chain around his neck and thought it must be a new piece of jewelry he wasn't used to yet. Since he often wore a suit or at least a sport jacket, she hadn't thought he was wearing anything but a chain. Fitz had always gone for flashy gold accessories from his expensive watch to his diamond pinkie ring.

"What kind of thumb drive?" she asked.

"Silver, thin, one of those new ones," Edwin said.

"Thank you for telling me about this," she said.

Silence, then, "I had to tell him that you came by and tried to get me to help you."

"I know."

"I—I…" She heard a noise in the background like a door opening. "I have to—" The last thing she heard was Edwin say, "What are you doing here?" before the phone went dead.

Bella quickly disconnected. Someone had walked in on Edwin. Had they overheard what he'd been saying? Her cell phone rang. Edwin? She didn't think so. She listened to it ring, hugging herself against the shudder that moved through her body. All her instincts told her not to answer the call because it wasn't Edwin calling from his number. It was whoever had walked in on him wanting to know who he'd called.

Now wide-awake, she leaned back against the headboard and looked across the room, her eyes unseeing. Was it true about the thumb drive? Even if it was, how was she going to get it from around Fitz's neck? Very carefully. Unless that had been Fitz who'd caught his father calling her. If he'd overheard what Edwin had told her, then he'd be waiting for her to try to steal the thumb drive hanging around his neck.

WHEN BILL MCMILLAN opened his eyes the next morning, Tommy was sitting in a chair beside the man's bed. "Hey," Tommy said.

He couldn't help feeling responsible for what had happened to the man. Apparently getting drunk at the bar and walking back to his apartment was a nightly thing. But Tommy kept thinking about how paranoid Bill had been about meeting him, afraid that Fitz would find him. Had he been followed? Had Fitz not just found his former accountant—but Tommy as well?

Last night when he reached the hospital, he'd finally checked his phone and saw the message from Bella. *Fitz knows. Be careful.*

Bill tried to smile. "Was I hit by a bus?"

"Pretty close. An SUV."

The man's gaze was unfocused for a moment, as if he was trying to remember. "An accident?" Tommy shook his head and Bill swore. "I have insurance."

Tommy thought he was talking about the hospital bill for a moment. Bill grimaced in pain as he said, "We had a deal. He broke it. Screw him. Get my insurance. It's hidden in my apartment under the floorboard in the bedroom. Get the bastard." Bill closed his eyes. "My apartment keys were in my jacket pocket. The hospital probably has them."

A nurse came in. "Mr. McMillan?" she said as she neared the bed. Bill's eyes opened. "A police officer is here who wants to ask you a few questions. Feel up to it?" Bill nodded.

Tommy rose. "I'll be going now, but I'll check back later."

Bill met his gaze and gave a small nod. "Thanks for taking care of things for me. My cat," he said, turning to the nurse. "He needs the key to my apartment so he can feed my cat."

The nurse nodded. "Your belongings are at the nurse's station." She turned to Tommy. "Just follow me. You'll have to sign the keys out," she told him as he followed the nurse down the hall.

"No problem." He called Bella and told her what had happened and where he was headed.

"Give me the address," she said. "I'll meet you there.

BELLA WAS STILL UPSET. The message Tommy had left on her phone last night just said he was fine and would talk to her today. This morning he'd filled her in on the accident. She knew he wasn't telling her everything. She'd been worried about him yesterday—and apparently with good reason.

He was waiting for her when she drove up. As she got out and glanced around, she couldn't help being surprised that the accountant lived just off this alley. She vaguely remembered seeing Bill McMillan at her father's office. As far as she knew, he'd made a good living but since being fired by Fitz, he seemed to have fallen on hard times.

Seeing her surprise, Tommy said, "He's been hiding out. I fear I led Fitz right to him and that's why he was almost killed. The police think it was an accident. Stolen SUV. Kids on a joyride."

"But you know better. This is a really narrow alley," she said, looking down it before turning to him again. She thought of Ronan and Milo. Fitz couldn't have been behind the wheel because he was at dinner with her. Was she his alibi? She felt sick to her stomach remembering him professing his undying love last night at the restaurant. She had wondered at his good mood. Now she thought she understood.

"It wasn't only the accountant Fitz was trying to kill," she said, but knew Tommy wasn't going to tell her what had really happened.

"This way," he said, no doubt thinking he was protecting her. As they walked he filled her in what Bill had told him. "He said he got fired. From what I gathered, he'd wanted more money on the deal. He did tell me that your father was so distracted that he signed anything Bill put in front of him."

Bella shook her head. "My father was always so trusting when it came to Edwin and Fitz. His first mistake. Add in his girlfriend Caroline… He really had no idea what was going on right under his nose." She was hesitant to tell him about Edwin's call and her dinner with Fitz. With luck they would find what they needed in Bill's apartment and put an end to this.

Tommy opened a heavy metal door with graffiti splashed across it and they stepped into a small landing at the bottom of a steep set of dark stairs. "It's number four," he said and started up, her close behind.

Their footsteps echoed as they climbed. She

could smell a variety of unpleasant scents as they passed several apartment doors. Behind them were the sounds of cooking, televisions turned up too loud and raised voices.

At number four, Tommy pulled out a key, but before he could use it, the door swung inward. Someone had already been here, she thought as she saw the ransacked apartment. Her heart fell. Whatever insurance Bill McMillan had hidden here had to be gone.

Tommy let out a low curse. "Wait here." He entered the residence, wading through the destruction toward what appeared to be the bedroom. The bed now leaned against the wall exposing the wooden floor. Several of the planks had been removed.

She watched him look into the gaping hole in the floor and then turn back to her in defeat, shaking his head. Fitz won again. That was all she could think about as they made their way back down the stairs to their vehicles.

They found a coffee shop and sat in a back corner. Bella cupped her mug in her hands, wishing she could chase away the cold that had settled inside her as she told Tommy first about dinner with Fitz and then the two thugs who'd been waiting for him in the parking lot.

"It sounded like he owed them money," she said.

Tommy shook his head. "I'm not surprised. Bill said that Fitz has been living beyond his means for some time. Once Bill did away with the shell com-

pany and that free money, he'd wondered what Fitz
had been doing for income to support his lifestyle
and gambling habit."

"We may know soon," she said and told him
about the call from Edwin this morning.

"A thumb drive?" he said when she'd finished.
"Bella, if it's around his neck—"

"I know. But I have to try," she said quickly.

He shook his head. "You can't be serious. If he
catches you—"

"How can it be any worse than what is happening right now?" she demanded. "He would just gloat
that he'd won again." She feared that he would do a
whole lot more, but she wasn't about to share that
with Tommy.

"I don't like it," he said.

She took a drink of her coffee and felt the heat
rush through her. "I don't like it either, but time is
running out. I have to try to get the thumb drive. If
Edwin is telling the truth—"

"Exactly. You sure Fitz didn't put him up to
this?"

Bella wasn't sure of anything except the impend-
ing wedding looming on the close horizon—and
what Fitz might do to her father before this was
over. What hung between her and Tommy was the
realization that Fitz had gone beyond just threatening people. He or one of the men he'd hired had tried
to kill the accountant and she was pretty sure the

driver had also tried to kill Tommy. Ronan? Miles? Either were capable, she thought.

"You know what scares me?" she asked, feeling the tightness in her chest as she realized that she'd underestimated Fitz. "Fitz is much more desperate than I thought. I should have realized it. He's buying drugs to frame my father, throwing this elaborate wedding, he's been stealing money from the partnership, he's blackmailing me and his father, and now attempted murder?" She looked up into Tommy's handsome face. "Now I suspect he not only knows about us, but that he had someone try to kill you last night. I can't see you anymore. I'm firing you."

As SHE STARTED to rise to leave, Tommy reached for her arm. "No," he said, easing her back into her chair. "Not happening. You aren't doing this alone." He knew Bella. She wouldn't give up. She would do this alone if she had to. But he wasn't going to let that happen—even as much as he wished he could talk her out of doing anything dangerous.

"You're right. He's become more desperate." He met her gaze. "I know he wants you, but there has to be more. You're just part of the plan. I need to ask you something. How much money do you have?"

She blinked. "On me right now?"

"No," he said with a shake of his head. "What are you worth?"

"You think Fitz wants my money." She laughed. "I think you're right. I know he wants the ranch."

He twined his fingers in her hand. "I'm in this with you whether you fire me or not." He thought about Margo and the unpaid rent. Maybe Fitz could no longer afford her. Or no longer needed her. Either way, Fitz was getting more desperate, which meant he was getting more dangerous.

"So what's your plan to get the thumb drive?" he asked, knowing that she would try no matter what he said. He saw at once from her expression that she hadn't had a plan. "You're going to need some strong sedatives. I'll get them for you. What does this thumb drive look like?"

"Silver, thin," she said, her voice breaking as her eyes welled with tears. "Thank you. I'll need one like it to replace the one I take."

He nodded. "I'll get it," he said, his voice also filled with emotion. He couldn't bear the thought that he might get this woman killed. "We do this together. Just like when we were kids."

She nodded and wiped at her tears. "Please be—"

"Careful? Have you forgotten that as soon as my license comes back I'm going to be a private investigator? *Trouble* is my middle name now."

"That isn't funny."

"But it's true," he said, squeezing her hand. She was shaking and he knew that she was scared. For him.

He had to bite his tongue not to tell her how

much he loved her. But damned if he would do it in some coffee shop. When this was over…

"I'll bring the sedatives and the thumb drive," he said, trying to hide how terrified he was of what Fitz would do if he caught her. "Can you meet me later at that old pine where we used to ride our horses?" She nodded. "You're sure you can get away?"

"He's still letting me ride my horse," she said through gritted teeth. It more than grated on her that he had moved in and thought he could tell her what to do. Unfortunately, he could. For now. "Later this afternoon before sundown?"

"I'll be there. I'll come by horseback."

THE COLT PROPERTY was large but because it wasn't on the river, it wasn't worth as much as the Worthington ranch. Still, Tommy loved the land his great-grandfather had bought but never built on. All of them had spent so little time in Lonesome that building a house had remained a pipe dream.

Until James came home and fell in love with Lorelei. The house was coming along nicely. One of the first things James had done was fence off some pasture and build a stable and corral for their horses. Tommy had been keeping his horse and tack out here since he'd returned home.

After saddling his horse, he rode up over the mountain to drop down toward the river. The large pine he and Bella used to climb when they were kids was in the far corner of the Worthington ranch far from any roads—right next door to Colt land. It was very private since there were no roads into it—another reason it had been one his and Bella's favorite places to hang out as kids. While their parents knew about the tree house, they didn't know about the other spots they went to. No one found them here because no one came this far to look for them.

He spotted Bella's horse tied up some distance from the tree and reined in. As he swung out of the saddle, he saw her waiting for him under the mighty limbs of the old pine. She'd spread out a horse blanket and now sat with her back against the tree trunk. The waning sun shone on her face as he tied up his horse and walked toward her.

She looked so beautiful it choked him up. He realized he couldn't wait any longer to tell her how he felt. He'd held it in for too long. Her gaze tracked him, the expression on her face intrigued—and expectant. He chuckled to himself. Bella was too sharp not to know how he felt—or why he'd wanted to meet here. Had she, like him, been waiting for this day?

## Chapter Eighteen

Bella studied the good-looking, dark-haired cowboy headed her way and felt her heart bump in her chest. His expression stole her breath. His long legs, clad in denim, quickly covered the distance between them.

She pushed to her feet, feeling the air tingle around her like dry lightning. Tommy didn't speak, just took her shoulders in his large hands and pulled her into a kiss. She felt the electricity popping around her, felt the spark as his lips touched her. It sent a jolt through her, straight to her middle, as he backed her up against the smooth tree trunk and she wrapped her arms around his waist and brought him closer.

He made a sound deep in his throat as one hand dropped to her breast. She groaned against his mouth as he slipped his hand inside her shirt and under the cup of her bra to fondle her now granite-hard nipple. He caught the tip between his thumb and finger and gently rolled it back and forth.

She arched against him, a groan coming from her lips. Only then did he pull back from the kiss to look into her eyes. She saw the desire burning there as hot as his callused fingers still teasing her aching nipple.

"Tell me to stop," he said, his voice hoarse with obvious emotion.

She shook her head. "I've wanted this for way too long."

The words appeared to be his undoing. He swept her into his arms and gently laid her on the blanket she'd spread out for them. For a moment, he merely stared down into her face. She smiled up at him, and then taking his face in her hands pulled him down for a kiss.

After that, Bella vaguely remembered the flurry of clothing flying into piles on the blanket before they rolled around, both naked as jaybirds. She'd known that their lovemaking would be both wild and playful—just as they had always been. She wasn't disappointed.

She'd never wanted anything more than she wanted Tommy as she began to feel an urgency. She desperately wanted him inside her. He bent to lathe each hard nipple with his tongue before trailing kisses across her flat stomach to her center. She moaned against his incredible mouth as he lifted her higher and higher until she thought she would burst. Until she felt a release that left her weak and shaking.

She drew him up to her, still desperately needing to feel his body on hers, in hers. The weight of him, the look in his eyes, the warm summer evening's breeze caressing their naked bodies. Hadn't she always known that if she and Tommy ever got past just being friends, this is where it would happen?

He started to speak, but she pressed a finger to his lips and shook her head. If he told her that he loved her right now, she feared she wouldn't be able to hold back the tears. She hadn't let herself admit how afraid she was that they couldn't stop Fitz.

She guided him into her and began to move slowly, her gaze locked with his. Their movements grew stronger, faster, harder. She arched against him, filled with a desire that only he could quench. When the release came it was powerful. Pleasure washed through her as she rose to meet him again and again, before they both collapsed together, breathing hard.

"I knew it would be like that," she said as she looked into his pale blue eyes.

"Bella—" She slipped from his arms. "Come on." Reaching back, she took his hand and pulled him up to run toward the river where it pooled among the rocks. The sun was all but hidden behind the mountain and yet the evening was summertime warm as they ran into the water, laughing. Droplets rose in the summer air and seemed to hang there.

Bella filed it all away in a special place in her

heart, memorizing the scents, the light, the feel of the water and Tommy for fear this was all they may get when the dust settled.

LATER TOMMY WOULD remember the water droplets caught in her lashes. Her laughter carrying across the water. She hadn't let him tell her how much he loved her. But she knew. He'd seen that moment of fear in her eyes and felt it heart deep. They had no future unless Fitz could be stopped.

It was the only thing on his mind as he rode his horse back to his brother's place. He and Bella had air-dried off in the evening warmth before dressing and riding off in different directions.

He'd given her the sedatives and thumb drive. "Call me when you can," was all he'd said. There was no reason to warn her to be careful. Or to try to change her mind about what she planned to do. The wedding was approaching too quickly.

"Don't come to the ranch," she warned him as she swung up into the saddle. "The place is crawling with the men he hired."

"How will you get me the thumb drive?"

"We'll meet tomorrow morning. Ten o'clock. At the fire tower."

"And if you don't make it?" he asked.

"I'll find a way to call you." She'd known that wasn't what he was asking, but he let it go. "Just don't try to come to the ranch. I'll get the thumb drive and find a way to get it to you."

He thought of their lovemaking and ached to feel her body nestled against his. He recalled the pale light on her skin and trailing a finger through the river water that pooled on her flat stomach before they made love a second time.

What terrified him was the way they'd parted as if they might never see each other again.

"Your bouquet," he'd said before she could ride away. "If things go wrong, there will be something in the roses from me."

Her eyes had widened but then she'd nodded. Neither one of them wanted this to go that far. But in case it did… "Thank you. I'll see you tomorrow."

## Chapter Nineteen

Bella fingered the small packet of crushed sedatives in her pocket for a moment before she took her seat at the dining room table across from Fitz.

She felt flushed from being with Tommy Colt and feared it showed on her face. If Fitz had known where she'd been and what she'd done… But if he'd noticed a change in her, he didn't show it.

"To marriage," Fitz said, lifting his full wine-glass. She hesitated to raise her own glass that he'd already filled. She didn't want to drink to-night. Later, she would need to be completely sober, completely in touch with her every movement if she hoped to succeed, because there was no way she wasn't going through with this.

"To truth and justice," she said and raised her glass, holding his gaze.

He laughed. "Whatever." He took a long drink. He seemed to be in a good mood…for some reason. Which concerned her.

She pretended to take a sip and put down her

glass. Roberto brought out their meals. She ate distractedly. Fitz ate with gusto, as if he hadn't eaten all day. He probably hadn't. She watched him out of the corner of her eye.

All she could think was that she needed a distraction so she could get the powder into his wineglass, but he seemed settled in, his gaze on her when he wasn't shoveling food into his mouth. Did he know what she planned to do? Had Edwin confessed that he'd told her about the thumb drive?

Fitz's cell phone rang, making her start and him swear. She had to relax. If he noticed how tense she was—

"I have to take this," he said and, dropping his napkin onto his empty plate, excused himself to head for the den. "What?" he demanded into the phone before he closed the door behind him.

She had no idea how long she had. Maybe only a few seconds. Quickly, she pulled the packet with the pulverized sedatives from her pocket. It took way too long to get the packet open, her fingers refusing to cooperate. She could hear Fitz still on the phone, but he was trying to keep the call short. He could open that door any moment and catch her. She feared she wouldn't get another chance tonight.

The bag finally opened. She poured the contents into his wineglass. Some of the white powder stuck to the side. She hurriedly poured some of her wine into his glass and swirled it around, spilling a little on the tablecloth.

She heard the door open and Fitz's raised voice. "We're in the middle of dinner," he said into the phone, the door opened a crack. "We can talk about this tomorrow."

All she could do was cover the spot with his plate, moving it though from where he had it set perfectly in front of him. Would he notice? He might. She moved the plate back to where it had been. Or at least close.

As he came out of the den, she reached for the wine bottle to refill her glass. Then she began to pour more wine into his glass, spilling just a little on the already stained tablecloth.

Fitz grabbed the wine bottle from her hand. "Clumsy. That's not like you." His heated gaze burned her as he walked around the table. Picking up his cloth napkin, he covered the spilled spot on the tablecloth and called for Roberto to bring him another napkin and take their empty plates.

She could feel his eyes on her, suspicious. The two spots on the tablecloth. He would see it. He would know. She looked up at him. He looked disgruntled with her. Would he demand the tablecloth be changed just to show that he was still in charge?

He took a deep breath, let it out and finally sat down. As he did, he straightened the salt and pepper shakers. She hadn't realized that she'd knocked over the salt in her hurry to cover up her crime.

She picked up her wine and pretended to take a

drink. Had she gotten away with it? Not until he drank his wine.

Roberto whisked away their plates, promising to return with a surprise dessert. She saw Fitz open his mouth as if to say he didn't want dessert.

"I do, please," she said quickly, cutting him off. Then she looked at Fitz and said, "I've been thinking." She lowered her eyelashes.

"Oh?" From under her lashes, she saw him pick up his wineglass and take a drink as he watched her.

"Maybe we could make a deal."

He chuckled. "You really aren't in a dealing position."

She met his gaze, ran her finger along the rim of her wineglass and wet her lips. She had his attention. More than that, she saw something in his eyes that surprised her. Yes, he wanted to punish her, destroy her, but he also wanted her as well as her ranch. His look was lustful. Maybe she had more to bargain with than he wanted to admit.

She took a sip of her wine and this time swallowed it. *Easy, girl. If this works, you need to be dead sober.* She continued to hold her wineglass. She'd heard somewhere that diners often mirrored their dinner companions. Reach for bread, they were apt to as well. Same with drinking?

Bella realized there must be some truth to it because Fitz took a healthy drink of his wine. She needed him to finish it, though. He was a big man. But there'd been enough sedatives in the packet to put down a farm animal. If he finished his wine-glass, he should start feeling the effects fairly soon.

But not too soon, she hoped.

"So?" he asked. "What is this...deal you want to make?"

She could see that he was interested, and it had gotten his mind off the spilled wine on the table-cloth. "I feel like we should call a truce."

He grinned. "A truce? What do you have in mind?"

She took another sip of her wine. She could feel the heat of it rush to her chest. But she had to get him to drink all of his. He had put his wine down but now picked it up again and nearly drained the glass.

She noticed with a jolt that there was white powder in the bottom of his glass. "It's going to take more wine," she said with a little laugh and reached for the bottle, knocking it over. There wasn't much left to spill but enough to cause him to leap to his feet as the bottle banged into his glass, spilling the last of the contents onto the already soiled tablecloth and running like a river straight for him.

He swore and jumped back just as she'd hoped. He didn't want to get red wine on his linen trousers.

She leaped up as well and grabbed his glass and spilled hers as well. "Roberto," she called. "We need help." She giggled as she felt Fitz's hard suspicious gaze on her again. "We're going to need another bottle of wine," she said, laughing as Roberto came into the room.

"I believe you've had enough," Fitz said. "Clean this up." He stepped back from the huge red stain on the white tablecloth as if it were blood.

Squeamish a little? She swayed and pretended to have trouble focusing. "I think we should discontinue this conversation for the moment. I might have to lie down or throw up," Bella said and grabbed the edge of the table for support. Had he noticed that her wineglass was less empty than his?

She told herself to be careful. Fitz watched everything. If he thought that she wasn't as tipsy as she was... Or worse, that she'd put something in his wine...

Roberto appeared and quickly took the dishes and the stained tablecloth. He saw that they were both standing and neither of them had sat back down. "No dessert?" he asked, sounding disappointed. "I made something special—"

She cut him off before he could say what. "Save me some please, but I really have to..." She didn't finish, just exited quickly, hurrying up the stairs to her room where she locked the door behind her.

Her back against the door, she stood listening until she heard Fitz's footfalls. Then she made gagging sounds until the footfalls quickly faded back down the hallway in the direction of the guest hallway.

Going to the intercom, she called down to the kitchen. "Roberto, I could really use some hot black coffee."

"And maybe dessert?" He lowered his voice and smiled. "I made tres leches."

She couldn't help but smile. "Why not?"

A few moments later there was a tap at her door. She couldn't be sure that Fitz hadn't waylaid Roberto and she would find him standing outside her door holding the tray, waiting to be let into her room.

She grabbed a towel, wrapped it around her head and splashed water on her face. As she was leaving the bathroom, she remembered to flush the toilet.

Unlocking the door, she opened it a crack. To her relief, Roberto was holding the tray. She stepped back to let him enter.

"Thank you," she said. "I don't feel so well."

"There are some over-the-counter pain relievers on the tray as well," he said and smiled as he quickly left.

She locked the door and reached for the coffee. If the sedative worked, then Fitz should be feeling the effects right now. She glanced at the time. She'd give it another fifteen minutes.

## Chapter Twenty

Tommy had taken his suspicions about Fitz's gambling debt to his brother James. It hadn't taken long before they had a completely different picture of Edwin Fitzgerald Mattson the Third. "He's in trouble. His lifestyle seems to have caught up with him."

"The car is leased," James said. "He's behind in his apartment rent and his credit cards are maxed out. Have you seen the wedding invitations?" He shook his head. "Cash-only gifts as the couple will be moving overseas."

Tommy swore and snatched the invitation out of his brother's hand. Did Bella know about this? He didn't think so. But since she wasn't planning to go through with the wedding, maybe she wasn't worried about it.

"So he does plan to sell everything, including the ranch," Tommy said. "Even taking all of this into consideration, it still seems like Fitz is too desperate."

James nodded. "I saw the police report on the

hit-and-run. I have a friend in the police department. You didn't mention that the bastard tried to kill you first."

"If it was Fitz's doing. Did your cop friend also tell you that the SUV was stolen and that they suspect it was an accident?"

"Yeah, like either of us believe that. Still, you're right. Fitz wouldn't know how to steal a vehicle unless the keys were in the ignition."

"There's more going on here," Tommy said. "From what Bella told me, he's gotten involved with the wrong people." James nodded. "I think this might have started with him wanting Bella, but that he now needs her money. The ranch is in her name. With the way things are selling in Montana right now…"

"That place is worth a small fortune, being on the river with the main house, bunkhouse, stable, new barn and all that land," James said.

"She has a couple of trust funds and some other money as well," Tommy told him.

"If Fitz is as desperate as it seems, he'll be even more dangerous," James said.

"That's what has me terrified, because of what Bella has planned." He couldn't sit still. How could he let her go through with this? How could he stop her?

"It's Bella," his brother said at seeing how anxious he was. "I'd put my money on her any day of the week to come out a winner."

Tommy smiled at his older brother. "I can't help but be scared. I don't know what Fitz will do next. He's already proven how dangerous he is."

BELLA POCKETED THE empty thumb drive Tommy had given her to replace Fitz's. If she didn't switch them, then he would know too quickly that his was gone. She needed time to find out what was on the drive before he realized what she'd done.

That was of course if she could pull this off. She checked the time. Now or never. Taking a deep breath, she unlocked her bedroom door, peered out.

The hallway was empty. This time of night most of the security guards were either at the bunkhouse or outside on the grounds. Not that one of them couldn't appear at any time in the hallway since she knew that they also made sure the house was secure.

She let her bedroom door close softly behind her before starting down the hallway in her stocking feet. The house seemed unusually quiet tonight. The moon would be up soon. But right now, it was dark outside, even with a zillion stars glittering over the tops of the trees. Shadows hunkered in the depths of the pines. Not a breeze stirred the boughs.

At the guest room wing she stopped to listen. She heard nothing but the pounding of her own pulse, as if the house were holding its breath.

Making her way down the short hallway, she stopped a few feet from his door and listened before she pulled out her passkey. As quietly as possible, she stepped to the door and slipped the passkey into the lock.

Breath held, she listened as she turned the key. It made a faint tick of a sound. She waited and then turned the knob and slowly eased open the door, terrified to think that Fitz could be lying in wait and about to ambush her.

The room was filled with pitch-black darkness. The drapes were partially closed. Faint starlight cut through the gap to cast a dagger-like sheen on the carpet. The room held a chest of drawers and a king-size bed with a club chair and two end tables. The door to the bathroom stood open, its interior also dark.

Over the thunder of her heart, she heard it. The sound of heavy rhythmic snoring came from the direction of the bed. She tried to breathe for a moment. She was shaking. If she hoped to get the thumb drive, she had to calm down.

Stepping in on her tiptoes, she let the door close quietly behind her and moved toward the bed and the snoring man sprawled there. With each step, she expected him to bolt upright. Surprise! Maybe the sedatives hadn't been powerful enough. Or maybe he hadn't drank enough. She tried to remember how much white sediment had been in the bottom of the wineglass.

She neared the bed, ready at any point to turn and run. It wasn't until she was next to the bed that she saw Fitz had lain down with all his clothes on.

The way he was sprawled, it appeared he'd barely made it before passing out. She wondered how fast the sedative had hit him and whether he'd realized what was happening before he hit the bed.

Bella told herself that she couldn't worry about that right now. Once she had the thumb drive, once she got it to Tommy, then it wouldn't matter what Fitz suspected let alone what he knew.

But because she didn't know how long it would take or even how she was going to get the drive to him, she had to replace the drive with the empty one.

Edging closer she listened to his snores. He lay on his back, one arm thrown over his head, the other lying across his rising and falling chest.

The moon rose up over the mountains, over the tops of the pines, the bright light fingering through boughs to shine through the space behind the partially opened drapes. That dagger of faint light was now a river of gold that splashed across the room.

The light glinted off the chain around Fitz's neck.

TOMMY PACED THE floor, unable to sleep. He should have talked Bella out of this. That thought made him laugh. Once Bella made up her mind… Still, he had to know what was happening out at the ranch.

His cell phone rang, making him jump. Bella? He snatched up the phone. "Hello?"

"Tommy, it's James."

His heart jumped into this throat. He couldn't speak, couldn't breathe. He gripped the phone, terrified of what his brother would say next. "Edwin senior is dead."

It took a moment before the unexpected news registered. "What?"

"I just got the call here at the office from my friend with the Missoula police," James said. "Apparently it was suicide. They think he's been dead since sometime yesterday."

Tommy didn't know what to say. He recalled Bella telling him about Edwin's call to her. She'd said someone had come in. She'd feared it was Fitz and that he might have heard what his father had told her. "Does Bella know?" he asked. "What about Fitz?"

"I have no idea if he's gotten the call yet. Can't imagine why anyone would call Bella."

But they would try to reach Fitz. Tonight. And given what Bella might be doing at this very moment...

"Bella's in trouble," he told his brother and explained about her plan.

James swore. "That's a bonehead idea if I ever heard one, but if anyone can pull it off it is Bella."

"If you're just trying to make me feel better—"

"I'm not. You know her. I'm sure you tried to stop her without any luck, right?"

"Right."

"What's the worst that can happen?" James said. "He wakes up and catches her. He isn't going to kill her. He can't."

"I hope you're right." But Tommy knew that if Fitz caught her trying to steal the thumb drive, he would make her life even more miserable and God only knew what he'd do to her father.

BELLA EDGED CLOSER to the bed. Her chest hurt from holding her breath. She let it out in a soft sigh as she kept her gaze on the bed and the man lying on it. Fitz hadn't moved. He continued to snore loudly. She assured herself that he couldn't hear her.

But once she touched him…

Her plan was simple. She would gently lift the chain at his neck. Except as she reached down, he let out a sharp snore and stirred. She froze. There was nothing else she could do. What would she do if he caught her? A half dozen lies flitted through her brain, all of them so lame they were laughable.

After a few moments Fitz fell back into more rhythmic snores again. She shook out her hand, her fingers tingling as if asleep. Then she reached down and with slow, careful movements, pinched the thick gold chain between her fingers. Slowly, she began to lift it.

As she did, she could see the shape of the thin thumb drive moving beneath his shirt as it headed for the V opening at this throat. Her mind started to play tricks on her, telling her that he was faking it, that he'd been expecting her, that once the thumb drive was visible his eyes would flash open and he'd grab her by the throat.

Her hand trembled and she had to stop for a moment. *Almost there, don't give up now.* She felt an urgency and yet she still pulled the chain slowly until she'd eased the thumb drive out from the shirt opening. It lay against his bare throat for a moment. She drew it over onto his shirt and let out the breath she'd been holding.

Now it was just a matter of unhooking the golden chain from around his neck. Hanging onto the thumb drive, she pulled on the chain until the clasp was reachable.

But in order to unhook the clasp, she had to lean forward over him closer than she'd ever wanted to be. She could smell his cologne and their long-ago-consumed dinner on his breath and tried not to gag. Her fingers shook with nerves. She tried not to look at his face as she worked at the clasp and yet she was still expecting his eyes to flash open, his hand to grab hold of her wrist. She was still expecting to be caught.

The chain came unhooked so quickly that she dropped one end of it. She hurriedly slipped off the thumb drive and pulled the new empty one from her pocket—and switched them. Now all she had to do was reconnect the clasp.

The whole process felt like it had taken too long and yet she knew it had only been a few minutes. Would Fitz be suspicious when he woke up to find his chain pulled out? She thought about trying to stick the thumb drive back under his shirt and was still considering it when his cell phone, right beside the bed, rang.

The sound was so loud in the room that she jumped and dropped the chain as she lurched back. Her gaze shot to his face. He'd stopped snoring. His eyelids fluttered.

*Move!* But her feet felt nailed to the floor.

The cell phone rang again. She took a step backward, then another and another, all the time watching his face as he attempted to drag himself up from the drugged sleep. She was to the door when she heard the phone stop ringing. She could only see the end of the bed from here.

Had he answered it? Her heart was pounding so hard she couldn't be sure. She eased open the door and stepped into the hall, pulling it gently closed behind her.

In those few seconds, she'd expected him to yank open the door and grab her. Inside his room, his phone began to ring again. Her heart banging like cymbals against her ribs, she turned and took off down the hall. At the end, she finally had the courage to look back—fearful that if she turned she'd find Fitz right behind her.

The hallway was empty, but she could hear someone coming up the stairs. She hurried down to her room, unlocked the door with trembling fingers and stepped inside. It wasn't until she had the door locked behind her and stood, trying to catch her breath, that she heard banging.

Someone was pounding on Fitz's door. In the distance, she could hear another cell phone ringing. She hurried to hers where she'd thankfully left it next to her bed. But as she picked it up to call Tommy, she heard a noise outside her bedroom door and then a knock.

"Bella?"

She recognized the voice. Ronan. The other guards called her Miss Worthington. He knocked again. She waited realizing she was supposed to be asleep. "Yes, what is it?" she called, hoping she sounded as if she'd just woken up.

"There's been an accident," Ronan called through the door. "Open up."

She reached for her robe, pulling it around her and hiding her clothes under it. "What kind of accident?" She could hear him waiting. She looked around the room clutching her cell phone. The thumb drive was in her jeans pocket under the robe.

At the door, she eased it open a crack. "What is it?" She sounded as impatient as she felt. She could hear Fitz's phone still ringing. Something had happened, that much was obvious.

"It's Edwin Mattson. He's dead. Suicide," Ronan said. His dark eyes bored into her.

She pulled the collar of her robe tighter. "Does Fitz know?" she asked.

"I thought you would want to know. Your fiancé is going to need you." There was censure in his words, in the look in his eyes.

Bella felt sick to her stomach. What did Ronan know? But when she met his gaze, she realized he was probably the one who'd followed her and Tommy to the river. He knew. So Fitz knew as well—just as she'd feared. "I need to get dressed." She slammed the door and quickly locked it an instant before he raised his hand to stop her.

She leaned against the door. Just minutes before she'd been home free. She had the thumb drive. She'd done it. Now this? Edwin? Suicide. A feeling of doom washed over her, making it even more difficult to breathe. She'd heard someone interrupt her call with Edwin. Had it been suicide?

This might change everything, she realized. What if she couldn't meet Tommy at ten at the fire tower? She held her cell phone to her chest remembering their lovemaking at the old pine tree. As badly as she needed to hear his voice, she realized she couldn't chance calling him. She could hear more footfalls in the hallway. Ronan could be standing out there listening.

No, she'd just find a way to meet Tommy at the fire tower and give him the thumb drive. In the meantime, it sounded as if the guards had managed to awaken Fitz. She needed to change clothes and go downstairs. The best thing she could do, she told herself, was to act as normally as possible. It wouldn't be hard to appear shocked about Edwin's death. It would be much harder to accept that he'd committed suicide—and hide her true fear that Fitz was behind it.

She closed her eyes, thinking of the man who'd tried to help her and her father. But mostly thinking of Edwin's call and the sound of someone interrupting them—someone he'd feared. His own son?

Dropping her cell phone into her purse, she hurried to her laptop and inserted the thumb drive. She might not have much time, but she needed to know that this wasn't another of Fitz's tricks and that there really was something on this drive.

She could hear the sound of footfalls in the house, the commotion mostly in the guest hallway. Had he realized by now that he'd been knocked out?

There was only one file on the thumb drive. She clicked on it just an instant before there was loud knocking at her door again. Data. Lots of data, everything she needed, she hoped. Edwin had told her the truth. Hurriedly, she ejected the thumb drive and pocketed it in her jeans.

"I'm getting dressed," she called through the door—not about to open it again. She didn't trust Ronan. That was the problem with mad dogs. Sometimes they even turned on their owners.

But this time the voice on the other side came from one of the other guards. "Mr. Mattson would like you to join him downstairs."

She glanced at the time. It would be daylight soon. What could Fitz want with her? "I'm getting dressed. Please tell him that I'll be down shortly."

She waited until she heard the man move away from the door before she hurried to change. Exhaustion pulled at her. It had been a nerve-racking night. She considered what to do with the thumb drive and decided keeping it on her was best. Her burner phone was in the car. She'd call Tommy on the way to the fire tower.

Dressed in a clean pair of jeans and a blouse, she pocketed the thumb drive, pulled on a jacket and went downstairs, taking her purse with her. As soon as she could, she'd go to Tommy.

Fitz was so adamant about them looking like a loving engaged couple, he would probably want her to go with him to talk to the police and make arrangements for his father's body to be taken to the funeral home.

But with Fitz she never knew what to expect. He could still be somewhat out of it because of the sedatives. She figured one look at him would tell her whether or not he knew what she'd been up to.

## Chapter Twenty-One

Fitz tried to think. His head felt filled with cotton. "Coffee," he demanded once Roberto had been awakened and sent to the kitchen. "Keep it coming." The police had called with the news. They would want to see him. But they couldn't see him in this condition.

He caught a glimpse of himself in a mirror in the dining room and recoiled. He couldn't meet with anyone looking like… He narrowed his gaze at his reflection. He hadn't consumed that much alcohol at dinner. No, the way he was feeling wasn't from the wine.

At the sound of footfalls, he turned to see his lovely future bride coming down the stairs. Every time he saw her, he was stunned at how perfect she was. She'd always been like this, even as a girl. So self-assured, so adorable, so capable of just about anything.

The reminder sent a stab of worry through him. He touched the chain at his neck. When he'd awakened fully clothed as if from the sleep of the dead, the chain and thumb drive had been outside his shirt. He'd hurriedly stuffed it back in as he'd gone to the door to find the guards standing in the hallway looking worried. Apparently they had been banging at his door for some time.

"Sir, your phone is ringing and the police are on the landline downstairs," one of his men had said, eyeing him strangely.

Fitz had had to fight to make sense of what the guard was saying. He'd turned back to his bed, shocked to see that he hadn't been under the covers. He hadn't even removed his clothing from last night. That was when he'd realized that his phone was ringing. He'd stumbled to the end table and grabbed up his phone. His father was dead. Suspected suicide?

He'd felt as if he'd missed more than a phone call. He'd lost hours of time and didn't have any idea how it had happened.

"I'm sorry to hear about your father," Bella said as she joined him.

He looked into her green eyes. It was like looking into a bottomless sea that beckoned him before the lids dropped, shutting him out. "Thank you," he said, his tongue feeling too large for his mouth. He turned and yelled into the kitchen. "Where is my damned coffee?"

"Let me go see," Bella said and started past him.

He grabbed her arm and shook his head. "Stay

here with me." His voice broke, surprising him. He sounded like a man who'd just lost his father. He was taking this much worse than he'd expected. He and Edwin senior had been at odds for so long now...

She didn't argue. "Would you like me to go with you to talk to the police?"

The offer touched him and made him suspicious at the same time. She looked guilty of something. He would eventually find out, he told himself. Right now just keeping his eyes open was hard enough. Thinking hurt. "Thank you," he said, knowing he had no intention of taking her up on her offer. He'd go alone. Bella had spoken to his father recently. He couldn't trust that she wouldn't say something that might cast suspicion on him.

Roberto hurried out of the kitchen with the coffee. Also on the tray along with the cups and spoons were what appeared to be small cakes and a bowl of strawberries.

"I thought you might like something while I make your breakfast," Roberto said.

Fitz was touched by the man's thoughtfulness, until he realized that the gesture wasn't for him. The cook was beaming at Bella. He waved Roberto away and pulled out Bella's chair. "It seems you have a not-so-secret admirer," he said as he shoved her chair hard into the table.

She let out an *ooft* that made him feel better as he moved to his chair and sat down. Bella had recovered quickly. She busied herself pouring him a cup of coffee. Yes, she definitely felt guilty about something, he thought. He couldn't wait to find out what. Something more than Tommy Colt?

Just the thought of her with that cowboy made him grit his teeth. His head ached with a dull constant throb. He couldn't make sense of why he felt so…sluggish.

Ronan came into the room and motioned that he needed to speak with him. Fitz shot a look at Bella. Did she suddenly look pale? He believed she did. What now? he thought as he rose and excused himself to go speak privately with the man.

BELLA SIPPED HER coffee and tried not to act interested in whatever Ronan was telling his boss. She couldn't hear what was being said, but she saw, out of the corner of her eye, Fitz turning around to look at her.

When he came back to the table, he apologized for the interruption and sat down. He seemed even more uncoordinated than usual, as if his balance was off from the sedatives. She saw him frowning as if trying to understand what was going on.

Whatever Ronan had told him had him upset. She could feel waves of anger coming off Fitz like electrical currents. She braced herself, knowing that whatever the guard had told him, it wasn't good. She thought about her lovemaking with Tommy yesterday evening. She'd been so sure that she hadn't been followed.

Helping herself to some strawberries and one of the small cakes, she offered to dish up a plate for Fitz. He growled under his breath and shook his head, hardly taking his eyes off her. The waiting was starting to get to her. Fitz sat rigid, staring a hole into her.

"I'm sure you're upset now that the wedding will have to be postponed," Bella said as she lifted her coffee cup to her lips.

Fitz roared, slamming his hand down on the table. Dishes and silverware rattled. His coffee slopped over onto the tablecloth, making him let out yet another oath.

He threw his napkin down on the stain as he appeared to fight for control. Was this about what Ronan had told him? Maybe his father's death had hit him harder than it had first appeared. Maybe he hadn't killed Edwin. Maybe it had been suicide after all and now it was interfering with Fitz's plans. Whatever the reason, his mood was worse than anything she'd seen before.

"Roberto," he called. "Please bring me another napkin." The cook responded at once and then quickly went back to making their breakfast plates. She watched Fitz carefully wipe coffee from the side and bottom of his cup before just as carefully folding the napkin and putting it aside.

One of his guards came into the room, stopping

at the end of the table. Her heart dropped as she saw what he held in his hands—her laptop computer. The man set it down and left.

She shot a look at Fitz. He had been watching for her reaction and was now smiling. Picking up his cup, he took a sip of coffee and then another. She knew that the sedatives were probably partially to blame for the man's mood—but not all of it. His face was now composed but she could see fury just beneath the surface. It wasn't just his father's death that had him so upset.

Bella tried to remain calm but as she took another sip of her coffee she had to hold the cup with both hands to hide her trembling. Had he plugged in the thumb drive around his neck and found it empty? If so, he would know that she'd switched them. In which case, he would also know that she'd drugged him last night, which would explain why he wasn't thinking clearly.

She knew he was waiting for her to ask about her laptop so she didn't. Roberto brought out their breakfasts and she dug in, even though she had to choke it down. She could feel Fitz's gaze on her as she ate and pretended that everything was fine. She could feel her pulse just below her skin thumping. How much did he know? And what would he do now?

What she'd found on the thumb drive was more than bank and business records. There had been bank account numbers and passcodes for three foreign banks. She hadn't had time to find out how much money might be in each, but she suspected the money might be more of an issue with him than her destroying his hold over her.

"We are not postponing the wedding," he said calmly. He held out his hand. She looked from it to his face, uncertain what he might want from her. "Give me your keys."

Bella instantly bristled. "I will not."

"I'm afraid you now have no choice. Your…behavior with Tommy Colt will no longer be permitted. You are *my* fiancée. As such you will no longer sneak off to have sex with another man." She started to speak but he talked over her. "You will not be allowed to leave this house until the wedding this Saturday. If that cowboy comes around, he will be shot."

"You can't hold me here," she said with more conviction than she felt and saw in his expression that he could and would keep her here. She was now his prisoner. She thought about the burner phone hidden in her car and the thumb drive in her pocket. Tommy would be waiting for her at the fire tower at ten.

"Give me your cell phone and your keys. I already have your laptop and I've had the landline disabled. I don't want to have one of my men frisk you any more than I want to have them tear your room apart, but I will."

She reached into her purse, took out her keys

and her phone and set them on the table, her mind racing. She had to get the thumb drive to Tommy. She had to at least call him. It would be just like him to come to the ranch if he didn't hear from her.

"What about your father?" she asked as Fitz reached across the table and scooped up her phone and keys. She'd actually thought that he'd been close to Edwin. But then again, Fitz had been blackmailing him—just as he had her father and her. Wasn't that why Edwin killed himself? If Fitz hadn't murdered him, she reminded herself. Edwin had turned on his son. If Fitz had been the person she'd heard in the background on the phone...

"His last wish was to be cremated," Fitz said. "Given that he killed himself, I think a quiet family-only memorial after we get back from our honeymoon would be best."

She met his gaze. "But we aren't coming back from our honeymoon."

He had the good grace to redden at being caught in one of his lies. "Why would you say that?"

"Because you've already made arrangements to sell the ranch while we're gone," she said.

"We won't need it any longer," he said, defensively.

"As your wife, I'd be glad if I had a say in what happens to my family ranch," she said, refusing to cow down to this man. She would never be his wife.

Fitz laughed. "You have no say in anything. Haven't you realized that by now? I have both you and your father exactly where I want the two of you. We will be married Saturday and if you do anything to embarrass me, both of you will regret it to your dying day. Am I making myself clear?"

She swallowed. Fitz had her laptop, her phone and her keys. Unless she could get the thumb drive to Tommy, then Fitz would win. She couldn't clear her father—and the wedding was only two days away.

## Chapter Twenty-Two

Tommy had been waiting for word from Bella. He'd gone to the fire tower and waited an hour before returning to the office where he now paced. "She should have called by now." He hated to think what Fitz might have done if he'd caught her attempting to take the thumb drive last night. The not knowing was killing him.

"She probably couldn't get away because of Edwin's suicide," James told him. Tommy knew that could be the case. Or it could be something much worse. If Bella had the thumb drive, she would do whatever it took to get it to him.

When his cell phone rang, he jumped and quickly pulled it out, praying it was Bella. It wasn't. It was FBI agent Ian calling from back East.

"Our face recognition program identified Caroline Lansing," Ian said. "Her real name is Caroline Brooks. She's a con woman and wanted in numerous states for fleecing rich older men. But with the information you gave us, we might be able to pick her up before she does it again."

"What about retrieving his money?"

"Sorry, he'd have to wait in line. I'm sure the money is long gone. But I doubt she was working alone. We have a lead on her. I'll let you know once we have her in custody."

"I suspect she didn't find this mark by accident," Tommy said. "If so, it would help the case I'm working on. The man's name is Edwin Fitzgerald the Third, better known as Fitz."

"You're thinking she might want to make a deal. I'll let you know."

He disconnected, feeling even more anxious. If there were a connection between Caroline and Fitz, she might implicate Fitz for a lighter sentence. Tommy held on to that hope.

Right now, he was more worried about Bella. He didn't dare call her cell. He'd already tried the burner without any luck. He didn't dare keep calling it. His only hope was that with Edwin senior dead, Fitz would delay the wedding.

FITZ WAS AS good as his word when it came to locking her up inside the ranch house. She wasn't allowed to leave. A guard had been posted at each door— including her bedroom.

"Ronan and Miles give me the creeps," she'd told Fitz. "I don't want to see either of them outside my room. You do realize that neither of them can be trusted, don't you?"

He'd laughed at that. "Talk about the pot calling the kettle black."

She'd held her ground and had been relieved when she hadn't seen either of them around. But she'd known they were still on the ranch and that if she tried to escape, they would be the most dangerous to come across.

There was no escaping though and Fitz knew it.

"What am I supposed to do over the next two days?" she'd demanded. "Stay in my room?"

"That's a very good idea," he'd agreed. "That way I'll know you're safe."

She scoffed at that. "I won't be safe until you're out of my life and my father's."

Fitz looked hurt. "I'd hoped we were past that by now. I've asked you to marry me."

"You've blackmailed me, moved into my ranch, threatened me with armed guards and now you're holding me prisoner," she said. "Let's not pretend that you're the victim here."

"Neither are you," he snapped. "You want out?" He picked up his phone. "I'll call the auditor who will call the FBI. They've been looking for enough evidence to put your father away. When they arrest Nolan, they'll find the drugs." Fitz shrugged. "You've always had a choice, Bella. Your father was a fool. If you hate me so much, then let your father get the justice he deserves and you can walk away."

He knew she couldn't throw her father to the wolves, no matter what foolish mistakes he'd made. Fitz knew that she'd never had a choice. She had the thumb drive but unless she could get it to the authorities…

No, she'd realized that there was only one way out. "I want to check on my flowers," she said the morning before the wedding.

"Is that really necessary?"

She stared at him. "Do I really not get any say in the wedding?"

He studied her for a moment, then relented. She could tell that he was hopeful she was accepting their upcoming nuptials. He started to pass her his phone, but then thought better of it. Getting up from the table, he went into the den and, after a few minutes, came back with her phone.

Bella knew he wouldn't let her leave the room to call the florist and was grateful when he got a call that at least took him away from the table. He didn't go far.

She hurriedly made the call. Susie Harper was a friend of hers and Bella was relieved when she answered. "It's Bella. I wanted to check on the bouquet."

Susie was silent for a moment. "The one that was ordered for you?" Before Bella could clarify, her friend said, "Tommy told me what you needed. With his help, it is ready to his specifications. Unless you want to change—"

"No," she said quickly. He must be planning to have a note inside the bouquet for her. She could tell that her friend desperately wanted to ask what was going on. "Thank you so much for doing that for me. I'll come by soon and we'll go to lunch and have a long talk."

"I hope so," Susie said, worry in her voice.

"You're a lifesaver," Bella said and hung up as Fitz cut his call short and returned to the table.

"Did you get what you wanted?" he asked.

She handed back the phone before he snatched it from her. "At least I'll have the bouquet I want."

"But not the groom," he said and cursed under his breath before saying he would be going out. "Do I have to warn you not to try to leave?"

She said nothing, just glared at him, wondering what she would find in the bouquet tomorrow.

FITZ COULDN'T WAIT for the wedding. Soon he would have everything he wanted. As it turned out, his father had done him a favor by taking his life. The man must have realized that if Bella agreed to be married to his son, someone still had to take the fall for the legal and financial problems with the partnership. If Fitz kept his promise and didn't give the Feds the books that made Nolan guilty, then he had to make it appear that Edwin senior was behind everything. His father must have come to that same conclusion.

With Edwin senior dead, it would be easier to let Nolan off the hook—unless Bella did anything to stop the wedding, Fitz thought.

*But you aren't married yet*, he reminded himself as he looked across the table at his fiancée later that evening. The past couple of days had been hell. If looks could kill, he'd be a molten pile of ash on the floor. She hated him.

Still he held out hope that if he kept his promise, she might come to love him. It wasn't like she had a choice. Once they were married, if she didn't come around, then he would punish her in ways she couldn't yet imagine.

That wasn't really what he wanted, though. He was in love with her—in his own way. The thought made him angry since he knew she was in love with Tommy Colt. He'd ached for this woman for years. Now, he told himself, he would have her any way he had to take her. Just the thought of their wedding night made him shift in his chair to hide his desire for her.

In another twenty-four hours, she would be his.

"There is something I've wanted to tell you," he said. He'd hoped to tell her this when they got married, but thought maybe if she knew it might soften her feelings toward him enough that tomorrow would go smoothly.

Bella looked up at him. It was the first time he'd let her come downstairs to dine with him. Instead, he'd been sending up her meals to her room. He'd hoped being locked in her bedroom would bring her to heel. He should have known better.

But this evening, she'd looked surprised when he'd tapped on her door and invited her down to the dining room. At first, he'd seen that she'd been about to decline out of stubbornness. Clearly she'd been going a little crazy in her room for all this time.

"I wanted to talk to you about something," he'd told her, giving her a way to accept gracefully. Grudgingly she'd agreed to have their last dinner together before the wedding tomorrow at ten in the morning. He'd opted for a morning wedding because he couldn't bear waiting all day. This way they would have a brunch reception and slip away to start the honeymoon.

Roberto, of course, had made her something special for this last supper before the wedding. Bella had been polite with Roberto, thanking him and even sharing just enough small talk to have Fitz gritting his teeth. She could be so sweet to other people. To Fitz himself, she snarled like an angry dog. But he assured himself that if he had to, he'd beat that out of her.

Now she stopped eating to stare at him as if waiting patiently for whatever he had to tell her.

He took a breath, let it out slowly and smiled as he cleared his throat and said, "I fell in love with you the first time I saw you." No reaction. "Seriously, Bella, I love you." She started to speak, but he stopped her, afraid of what she might say to ruin this moment before he could finish. "I hate the way I've gone about this." He saw disbelief in her expression. "I would have loved to have simply asked you out, but I knew…" He let out a self-deprecating laugh. "With our history from childhood that you wouldn't have gone out with me."

BELLA WAS GLAD she hadn't spoken in the middle of his touching speech. She saw Fitz's vulnerability unmasked in his face, in the nervous way he kneaded at his cloth napkin, in the way his eyes shone. She warned herself to step very carefully.

"I'm sorry too that this happened the way it did," she said. She couldn't very well say that she was glad he'd finally shared his feelings. She wanted to tell him all the reasons she couldn't stand the sight of him. But that too wouldn't help right now.

"I had no idea that you felt like this," Bella said, thinking of his awful threats as to what he planned to do to her once they were married. Fitz had always struck out in anger from the time he was a boy.

She knew whatever she said next could bring out that anger in him and make things worse. But she wasn't sure how to make things better without lying to him and agreeing to marry him.

"I have to wonder…" She met his gaze. She felt her heart begin to pound. Careful. "Is this how you envisioned it going?"

"I'd hoped that if we spent time together maybe…"

"It's hard to force something like this," she said.

"But in time…" He still looked as if he really believed that she would come to love him once they were married.

"What if our feelings don't change?" she asked quietly.

He tossed his blond hair back and she saw the change in his expression. "You mean what if *your* feelings don't change."

"It would only cause us both pain."

When Fitz smiled, she saw the bully he'd been

as a boy and was now as a man. "I can promise it will be more painful for you."

Bella sighed and picked up her fork. Roberto had made her a special meal and she was bound and determined to do it justice. Also it was the first time she'd been out of her room.

She could feel Fitz's angry gaze on her and wondered how long it would be before he threw one of his tantrums. Fortunately, his phone rang. He let it ring three times before he shoved back his chair and stormed into the den to take the call. All she heard was him say, "I told you not to call me, Margo," before he slammed the door.

Bella looked toward the exits. Armed guards blocked both. She concentrated on her food. Tomorrow was the wedding. She'd found no way to get Tommy the thumb drive. She just hoped that whatever Tommy had put in her rose bouquet would save her.

Roberto came back to the table to see if she needed anything.

"Everything is wonderful, thank you," she said and dropped her voice. "Have you heard of anyone trying to get onto the ranch?" She saw the answer at once in his eyes. Her heart dropped and tears flooded her eyes. "Is he all right?"

The cook nodded. "I believe there was an altercation. Several of the guards needed to be patched up." He smiled then. "But when the sheriff came, the…intruder was escorted from the property."

Fitz came out of the den.

"Roberto was wondering if you needed anything else," Bella said, seeing that he suspected the two of them had been talking. The intruder would have been Tommy. She was so thankful that he was all right.

"I'm no longer hungry," Fitz snapped. "If you're finished, you should go back to your room. You need your rest. You're getting married tomorrow. I can have Ronan escort you." The threat had the exact effect he knew it would.

"I can see myself to my room." She rose and put down her napkin. "Roberto, thank you again for a lovely dinner," she called to the kitchen. With that she headed for the stairs.

Fitz followed her as far as the landing. He stood waiting as she entered her bedroom. A few moments later, she heard footfalls and then a key turned in the lock. She wanted to scream. Or at the very least cry.

But she did neither. She walked to the window and stared out at the ranch she loved, vowing she would do whatever it took tomorrow but she would never marry Fitz.

TOMMY'S ONE ATTEMPT to get onto the ranch and see Bella had been thwarted quickly. He'd known there would be guards. What he hadn't expected was to be accosted by two obvious thugs. He'd held his own in the fight even against two of them, but he was smart enough not to go back to the ranch alone.

As the wedding day had quickly approached, he'd become more concerned for Bella's safety.

"Fitz won't hurt her," James kept telling him. "He's planned this elaborate wedding and invited most of the county. If you're right and he's in love with her…he won't hurt her."

Tommy mostly agreed with James. "But we're talking Bella. She won't go through with it."

"How can she stop it?"

"That's what bothers me. I have no idea what she has planned," he said. "Fitz knows her, too. He'll be expecting her to do something. We have to stop the wedding before she does."

James sighed and nodded slowly. "You do realize that Fitz will also be expecting you to do something." He held up his hand before Tommy could argue. "I've already called Davey and Willie. They're coming in tonight. What we need is a plan."

Tommy nodded. "Whatever we do will be dangerous."

"I warned our brothers," James said. "This might surprise you, but they didn't hesitate even when I told them what we were up against."

The Colt brothers, Tommy thought as a lump formed in his throat. He'd always been able to depend on his brothers. But he'd never needed them as much as he did right now.

His cell phone rang. It was his friend with the

FBI. "Tell me you have good news," Tommy said into the phone. Right now, he'd take all he could get.

"We have Caroline. She is willing to give evidence against Edwin Fitzgerald Mattson the Third, or Fitz as you both call him," Ian said. "Apparently the two had crossed paths when she'd tried to latch on to his father. Fitz told her about Nolan and gave her inside information that helped her take all of his money."

"So you're going to arrest Fitz?" Tommy couldn't contain his excitement. "Right away?"

"Probably not until Monday."

"That will be too late," he told Ian. "Is there any way you can get some agents here tomorrow? Fitz is blackmailing Nolan's daughter into marrying him in the morning."

"I can try, but I wouldn't count on it. Have you talked to the local sheriff?"

"If Fitz had found out, he'd plant drugs on Nolan as part of the frame and blackmail. Bella was trying to get the evidence. But I've been unable to get near her the past couple of days. I'm really worried about her."

Ian sighed. "Let me see what I can do."

## Chapter Twenty-Three

The wedding day broke clear and sunny. Fitz had one of the guards bring her the wedding dress and shoes.

"Your attendants will be arriving soon," the guard said. "Mr. Mattson suggested that one of them help you get ready."

She thought about his controlling behavior and was surprised he hadn't tried to see her before the wedding. Instead he wanted to send someone up to make sure she got ready?

"No, I can manage," she told him. Fitz had chosen her attendants, women she knew but wasn't close to. Again optics. The women were ones who would look good in the wedding photos. "Tell Mr. Mattson that I'm fine."

She'd awakened with a start this morning, heart hammering. Getting up, she'd checked to make sure she still had the thumb drive. Her fear was that Fitz would check his and realize that they'd been switched. It wouldn't take much for him to find it in her room, no matter how well she hid it. That was why she kept it on her except when she was sleeping.

Fitz had kept her from seeing Tommy before the wedding. But she wanted to make sure the thumb drive got into the right hands depending on how things went in the next hour.

She'd showered, put on her makeup and fixed her hair, gathering it up into a do on top of her head. She had to look the part. Fitz still had time to call the cops on her father. Timing was everything, she told herself, wondering how she was going to be able to stop him. Was he planning on giving her the thumb drive around his neck before the ceremony?

Or would he break his promise and still turn in her father?

At the knock on the door, Bella stepped to it. "Yes?"

"Your bouquet has arrived," a male voice informed her.

She opened the door a crack and the guard handed her the tiny white rose bouquet. She took it and closed the door. Her heart pounded. Tommy knew her, knew she would be desperate. He had put something in the bouquet, she told herself. She'd heard something in her friend's voice who owned the floral shop.

Carefully parting the roses, Bella saw something glint silver at the center hidden deep in the roses. But it was the note, the paper rolled up into a thin tube tucked in among the petals, that she pulled out and quickly read.

"This is only a last resort," the note read. "I love you, Tommy."

Heart in her throat, tears in her eyes, she reached into the bouquet and pulled out the deadly-looking slim blade. She swallowed, nodding to herself. Tommy knew her, he loved her. He knew how desperate she was or she would have been in contact with him. He'd given her a sense of power, last resort or not. She carefully slipped the blade back in between the tiny white roses.

A knock at the door. She took one last look at herself in the full-length mirror. The perfect bride about to head down the aisle to the wrong man. She dabbed at her tears, willing herself that there would be no more. She couldn't think of Tommy, not now, because just as he knew her, she knew him. He would do everything in his power to stop this wedding. She had to be strong. She had to survive this—one way or another.

Another knock. This time it was Ronan's voice she heard just outside. He would be getting impatient to walk her over to the barn where all the wedding guests were waiting. She looked down at the bouquet in her hand knowing that when the time came, she couldn't hesitate.

She checked to make sure the thumb drive was still tucked securely under her garter. Over the past few days she would have done anything to get the drive to Tommy, but Fitz had made sure that she had no way to get away—or get a message to the man she loved.

Bella still didn't know if Fitz was aware that she'd switched the thumb drives. She told herself he'd been so busy with the wedding arrangements that he probably hadn't given it a thought.

Had he known he would have torn up her room looking for it. Or maybe he would have realized she could have hidden it anywhere in the house and that he might never be able to find it.

It didn't matter now. It was too late for either of them to do anything about it. She took a breath, knowing she couldn't put this off any longer. Fitz would be worried that she might pull something before the ceremony. She'd seen all the extra guards he'd hired outside the barn. They were for Tommy Colt. Fitz was so sure he'd thought of everything and that nothing could stop this wedding.

Bella opened the door. Ronan looked upset that she was taking so long. She stepped out, moving past him, ignoring him. But she could feel him behind her. His eyes burned into her back where the fabric of her wedding dress left her bare. The man frightened her under normal circumstances and these circumstances were far from normal.

They went downstairs and walked the short distance to the barn where the wedding was being held. Vehicles were parked everywhere. She let her gaze sweep over them, taking in all the guards.

Fitz had outdone himself and she suspected there would be even more on the way into the ranch—all to make sure that Tommy Colt couldn't get onto the property.

Her chest hurt at the thought of Tommy making another attempt to rescue her because if he did, she feared it would get him killed. She knew that Ronan and his friend Miles would have been ordered by Fitz to shoot to kill.

"Can't have any…trespassers on our wedding day," Fitz had said more than once over the past few days. "I'd hate to have any bloodshed. Ronan and Miles have promised to keep it at a minimum—unless necessary." The threat had been clear.

Bella thought of the blade in her bouquet. How ironic. *There would be bloodshed.*

As she and Ronan neared the barn, she heard the music and voices and spotted her attendants. They were all beautiful, slim and dressed in matching peach-colored gowns. Fitz had chosen well. Had there been photos of this wedding, they would have been quite gorgeous.

She gave the women a mere nod of her head as she stepped into the entry. The women had to be wondering why they'd been invited let alone why they weren't allowed to help the bride get ready for her big day.

Ronan moved past her to where her father was pacing nervously. He turned, looking both surprised and relieved to see her. He was dressed in a tux and looked quite handsome, she thought. He looked better than he had since she'd returned home, but he didn't meet her gaze as he came to stand next to her.

Bella stared straight ahead as she took his arm and waited as her attendants began the procession down the carpeted aisle between the seats that filled the barn to overflowing. A huge tent had been erected at the back of the house where Fitz had said the reception would be held.

He'd seemed disappointed that she hadn't wanted to see everything he'd arranged. She'd known she would never be going into the tent for the reception even before she'd seen the blade hidden in her bouquet.

"I'd rather be surprised," she'd told him. They hadn't spoken since dinner last night when Fitz had poured out his heart. She wondered if he really believed that he loved her or if it was just his excuse for what he was doing. Knowing that he was desperate for money, she figured that was more likely his true motivation.

But soon he thought he would have the ranch. With his father's death, he would have another third of the partnership. Or one hundred percent if he reneged on the deal and sent her father to prison.

He would however never have her, Bella told herself, knowing what she would do. Tommy had to have known how desperate she felt. That was why he'd seen to it that she had a way out.

Now as the attendants took their places, the aisle

opening up, she saw Fitz standing next to his best man and a group of handsome tuxedoed attendants. She met his gaze. The look in those blue eyes was one of appreciation as he took her in.

But there was also relief on his face. He'd been worried that Ronan would have to drag her to the altar. That would have definitely messed up his optics.

But that was the problem, wasn't it? He knew her. He had to know that she didn't trust him to destroy any evidence that would send her father to prison. Just as he had to know that she wasn't going through with this wedding no matter what he did.

Did he really think this barn full of people would stop her? The man was a fool. He'd lied, cheated and bullied his way to this point. It wasn't going to get him what he wanted. He didn't know the first thing about love.

But Bella did. Just the thought of Tommy made her stumble a little. Her father placed his free hand on hers. She could feel him looking at her. She didn't have to see his face to know there was fear there. He didn't want to go to prison. They both knew it would be a death sentence.

But had she looked at him, she knew there would also be regret in his eyes. This wasn't what he'd wanted for his daughter. It wasn't what he'd wanted for himself. He'd lost so much, his business, his money, his only daughter. No matter how this ended, he would be a broken man.

There was nothing she could do about that, she told herself. She had to think about her own survival—and keeping her father out of prison. The thumb drive under her garter would do that—once she was arrested.

Bella tried not to think about taking Fitz's life. She despised him but not enough to kill him under any other circumstances. He'd asked for this, but that still wouldn't make it easy.

He was still staring at her. She met his gaze and suddenly he looked nervous. She almost wished he had his usual smirk on his face. It would make things much easier.

As she reached him, her maid of honor started to reach for her bouquet. She shook her head and sniffed the roses as she joined Fitz. The music stopped. There was the racket of everyone sitting down. The preacher cleared his voice. She could feel Fitz's gaze on her face as she held the bouquet close, as if she couldn't part with it.

Would he insist she hand it to her maid of honor? Would he take it from her? She couldn't allow that. Glancing up, she saw his expression and knew that the time had come.

She pretended to touch the soft petals of the baby roses. Her fingers brushed over the cool steel of the knife. She looked up at Fitz and sunk her fingers into the roses.

FITZ COULDN'T HELP being nervous as he watched his soon-to-be bride fooling with her beautiful bouquet as if she were as nervous as he was. That gave him hope that she'd accepted the marriage. Accepted him.

It had taken her so long to appear that he'd worried that she'd somehow tricked Ronan and escaped. She wouldn't have gotten far—not with all the guards he had on the property—but it would have spoiled their wedding day. That was the last thing he wanted.

While he was waiting, he'd looked over the crowd. Anyone who was anybody was here today. He felt a sense of pride that they'd all come. But that little nagging voice in his head reminded him that they had come for Bella, not for him. Everyone loved Bella, he thought and tried not to grind his teeth.

He'd been worried about Nolan showing up, but the man looked like the quintessential father of the bride in his tux. He must realize that his life was now in his soon-to-be son-in-law's hands. Fitz hadn't decided if he would let Nolan off the hook or not. That was up to Bella.

He'd met her gaze as she'd headed down the aisle toward him. He'd tried to sense what she was thinking. Her face looked serene, too serene, and that bothered him. Did she look like a woman who knew she'd been bested and wasn't going to make trouble? He could only hope, but he knew that until the pastor declared them husband and wife, he was going to be holding his breath.

When her maid of honor reached for her bouquet,

Bella ignored her. Instead, she sniffed the tiny white roses before looking up at him. He'd seen something in her gaze that had threatened to loosen his bowels.

A shudder had moved through him as they'd locked eyes. His breath had caught in his throat and for an instant he'd felt…afraid. He swallowed now as he watched her fiddle with her bouquet. He tried to tell himself that she was merely nervous, something he'd never seen in her before.

He swallowed and was about to take the bouquet from her so they could get this over with when he heard a thunderous roar.

The guests heard it, too, he saw as he glanced toward the door. What in the world? He'd barely gathered his bearings when he recognized the sound. Horses. Dozens of them.

BELLA WOULD NEVER forget the look of panic and surprise on Fitz's face as the door to the barn burst open and Tommy came riding in on a horse. The horse thundered down the aisle through the barn between the seats, coming to a rearing stop before the altar. The moment Tommy reached for her, she swung up onto the back of the horse.

The barn broke out in pandemonium as the two of them rode toward the exit door—which was now blocked by Ronan. She saw the gun in his hand and the look on his face. She could hear Fitz screaming for Ronan to shoot to kill.

She pulled the knife from the bouquet and leaned

off to one side of the horse, drawing Ronan's attention. He hadn't seen the knife until she slammed it into him. Ronan's expression registered surprise as he dropped the gun and fell back. He got off one shot, but the bullet missed its mark, the report of the gunshot lost in the roar of horses and panicked screaming guests.

As she and Tommy Colt rode out of the barn, she tossed her bouquet over her shoulder. She didn't look back. The ranch yard was full of horses and riders. She recognized townspeople, neighbors, friends—who hadn't been invited to the wedding— all on horseback.

Some carried baseball bats. Others lengths of pipe. Most of the guards had backed down from what she could see. But Davy and Willie Colt were off their horses and involved in a fistfight with two of the guards.

The sound of sirens filled the air. Bella saw the sheriff and several more patrol cars roaring up the road. But Tommy didn't slow his horse as he headed into the woods at a gallop. She held on, wrapping her arms around his waist.

She looked back only once. Fitz stood in the barn doorway watching her ride away. The front of his tux was dark with what appeared to be blood. Had Fitz been hit by Ronan's stray bullet? Before she turned away, she saw him fall backward and disappear from view.

They hadn't ridden far when Tommy reined in

and helped her off the horse. He swung down beside her and took her in his arms. She leaned into him and for the first time in forever let herself breathe freely.

"You're all right now," Tommy said as he loosened her hair and let it drop to her shoulders. His fingers wound into her locks as he drew her to him. She finally felt tears of relief flood her eyes as she looked into his handsome face. Of course, he'd come to her rescue. Hadn't she known in her heart that he would do whatever he had to. As she had done what she had to. Together, they were one hell of a team.

"I got the thumb drive," she whispered as she turned her face up to him.

"I never doubted it," Tommy said, grinning at her as he dropped his mouth to hers for a kiss that quickly deepened.

At the sound of someone approaching, they drew apart and turned.

"You remember Ian?" Tommy asked. "He's with the FBI."

She nodded, then lifted the skirt of her dress and slipped the thumb drive from under her garter. "I think everything you need is on it," she said, holding it out to the agent. "I hope this will help put him away." If he wasn't dead already. "At least, I hope it will clear my father."

Ian nodded as he pocketed the thumb drive.

"They'll want a statement from you, probably at the Billings office."

"I'd be happy to give one," she said, surprised to hear her voice break. She'd come so close to taking Fitz's life. As it was, she'd stabbed a man. Ronan could be dead for all she knew.

Tommy put his arm around her and pulled her close. "Fitz?"

Ian nodded. "I heard he was shot. He's being taken to the hospital."

"One of his own guards I think shot him," Bella said, her legs feeling suddenly weak. She leaned into Tommy's strong body, loving the feel of his arm around her.

Everything had happened so fast. It now felt like a dream. She feared she would wake up only to find herself standing at the altar with Fitz, her fingers searching for the knife in her bouquet.

"Are you going to be all right?" the FBI agent asked.

She nodded as she looked up at Tommy's handsome, familiar face. For so long she'd feared that she might never see him again. Or that Fitz and his guards would kill him. She smiled at the loving look in his eyes and felt her heart float up. "I'm going to be fine."

## Chapter Twenty-Four

The next few days were a blur of cops, FBI and visits to the hospital where her father was recovering from a heart attack.

"I'm sure the stress played a major role," the doctor told her. "But he's recovering nicely. In fact, he's determined to get out of here as soon as possible."

Bella had been surprised by how quickly he'd recovered. When she entered his room later that week, she found him sitting up in bed. The change in him was nothing short of astounding. It was as if he was his old self again.

He smiled when he saw her. "Did the doctor say when I can get out of here?"

"He's keeping you a little longer." She studied her father and shook her head. He'd been so beat down before the wedding. Now though he looked ready to pick up the pieces of his life and move on as if nothing had happened. She wished she could put the past behind her that quickly.

"You and that Colt boy were brilliant," Nolan

said. "I really thought you were going to marry Fitz." He shook his head. "I should have known better." He should have, she thought as he reached for her hand and squeezed it. "You saved your old man. Strange the way things turn out. Edwin…" He let go of her hand and looked away for a moment. "The police think he really did commit suicide."

Bella had been told the same thing. Edwin was facing prison for his part in framing her father. But also he had to know that Fitz might let him take the fall for all of it. She wondered what it must have been like for him to realize that he couldn't trust his own son, and worse, that he held some responsibility for creating this monster.

"The company is mine now," her father said after a moment before he turned to look at her again. "With Edwin and Fitz gone…"

So he was no longer broke. "What will you do?"

"Rebuild it," he said without hesitation. "I did it once, I can do it again." He sounded excited about the prospect.

She wondered how much the bad publicity would hurt the business, but she figured her father wasn't worried. He liked a challenge. She told herself that he was smarter now, at least she hoped so.

"You know they caught Caroline."

He nodded and avoided her gaze. "I loved her." He shrugged. "I hadn't realized how lonely I was for female companionship. Maybe I'll find myself a nice woman. Or not," he said with a laugh. "But you don't have to worry about me anymore."

She hoped not. If Nolan did find a woman, Bella would have Tommy do a background check, she told herself.

Her father grew quiet and for a moment he looked his age. "I'm so sorry I put you in that horrible position I did."

"It's over," she told him, putting her hand on his shoulder. He covered her hand with his own for a moment. "But you're going to have to stop calling Tommy 'that Colt boy,'" she said, smiling. "After all, he's going to be your son-in-law."

Her father smiled, no surprise in his expression. "He's perfect for you."

She laughed. "Yes, he is."

## Chapter Twenty-Five

Fitz opened his eyes. For a moment, he couldn't remember where he was or what had happened. A hospital. A nurse came running, followed by a doctor.

It all came back to him as he started to move, only to realize there was a handcuff attached to his left wrist and the bed frame. He closed his eyes. He could hear voices around him, but he preferred the darkness of oblivion.

He'd come so close to getting what he wanted. Bella. Just the sound of her name in his head made him wince in pain. His breathing was already shallow. His chest ached with each attempt to draw in oxygen.

He suddenly felt for the chain and thumb drive around his neck. Gone! All of his gold jewelry. He realized the doctor would have removed it once he reached the hospital. Did that mean the cops already had it?

He closed his eyes, wishing that he'd died.

At a sound, he opened his eyes to find a man standing over him. His first guess? FBI.

"I'm FBI agent Ian Brooks," the man said. "I have a few questions."

Fitz shook his head. "I have nothing to say."

"We have your thumb drive and a statement from Bella Worthington," the agent said.

"You have no right to take my thumb drive," Fitz said. "That's my private property and should be locked up downstairs with my other personal items."

"The thumb drive on the gold chain, is that what you're referring to? No, that one's blank. I'm talking about the one Bella Worthington removed from the chain you kept around your neck."

Fitz felt his insides go liquid. "That's not possible." He thought of Bella. She would have had to— Like a flash of lightning, it hit him. "I have nothing to say to you," he said to the FBI agent. "I want my lawyer. Get out of my room. Now!"

"We'll talk soon," the agent said and left.

With a curse, Fitz knew how Bella had done it. She'd drugged him. That explained why he couldn't seem to wake up with the guards pounding at his door and the phone ringing to tell him that his father was dead.

He slammed his fists into the bed he lay in. The bitch. She'd taken the thumb drive. When had she gotten it to the FBI? He couldn't believe this. He'd kill her once he got out of here.

If he got out of here.

He closed his eyes, fighting panic. He would get out of here. Bella thought she was so much smarter than him. He'd show her.

At a noise right next to his bed, his eyes flew open. He'd expected to find the FBI agent back. But instead it was a pretty young nurse.

With a shock, he saw that she had green eyes. Her hair was blond, but he could imagine her as a brunette. She looked more like Bella than Margo. She was the right age though and her body wasn't bad. He smiled at her.

"I see you're feeling better," she said.

He was feeling better. Seeing this woman, he told himself it was a sign. This wasn't over. He would beat the rap against him. He would have what he deserved. "What's your name?" he asked.

"Roberta, but everyone calls me Bobbi."

"Bobbi." He whispered her name. "I like that." He rattled the handcuff on his wrist. "This isn't comfortable. It shouldn't be on there anyway. I didn't do anything wrong." He chuckled. "They got the wrong man. But once I'm out of here, I'll clear it all up." He'd hire a good lawyer. Or the best he could afford. So much of what the cops had against him was hearsay, his word against Bella's and her crooked father's. Even what was on the thumb drive he could explain away as Nolan trying to frame him.

"In the meantime," he said to the Bella-like nurse,

"if you could take off the handcuff—just so I can get some feeling back in my wrist…"

"I'm sorry, but it has to stay on except when you go for your MRI," she said, looking sympathetic. "I heard you were shot at your wedding?"

He nodded. "A terrible mistake. I can't wait to get out of this bed so I can clear it up. I was framed by a woman I thought I loved."

"I'm sorry," she said. "Now that you're better, I'm sure you can straighten it out."

"Oh, I will." He looked from her to the handcuff and then to the door. "What's the MRI for?" he asked.

"I'll let the doctor explain it to you," she said. "But don't worry."

He wasn't worried. Bella was the one who should be worried. Once he got out of here… He smiled at Bobbi and noticed she wasn't wearing a wedding ring. Not that it would have mattered. He would have her one way or another.

There was a noise out in the hallway. "I think they're ready for you," the pretty nurse said. "I'll have the officer come in now."

"Have you ever wanted to be brunette?" he asked.

She gave him a funny look but laughed. "Haven't you heard that blondes have more fun?"

Fitz chuckled. "Wait until you're a brunette and with me." Not that even this woman could satisfy his need for Bella. He would have them both. Only this time, he wasn't going to be so nice to Bella. He'd make her pay for this.

BELLA LOOKED UP at the sound of a vehicle. She'd spent a few days at Tommy's cabin by the river, not wanting to go back to the ranch yet. She told herself that the bad memories of Fitz would eventually fade. Tommy and his brothers had cleared all signs of Fitz from the ranch house, he'd told her, but she was happy being with Tommy out at the cabin. It was nice on the river. It was nice feeling safe and happy. She never wanted it to end.

But she had a business to run, and she'd decided to move the operation to the ranch. She had plenty of room there. And she couldn't hide out forever. Fortunately, when she'd walked in the front door, all the good memories of the place she loved came back in a rush.

Fitz was gone and forgotten. At least for a while. She'd heard that he was recovering from his gunshot but that when he'd collapsed from the wound at the barn that day, he'd hit his head. The doctor thought there might be some internal bleeding. She felt only glad that he was out of her life and tried not to worry what would happen if he were ever released from prison.

There was enough on the thumb drive to convict him of numerous felonies. Add to that kidnapping and blackmail and all that it entailed, and he shouldn't see freedom for a long time. He would hire the best lawyer he could. He would lie. She tried not to let that make her nervous.

Now she glanced out to see Tommy drive up

in his pickup. She felt a smile immediately pull at her lips. Just the sight of him made her happy. She opened the door, then froze as she saw his expression. "What is it?"

He led her over to one of the porch chairs and they sat. "It's Fitz. He was being taken to get an MRI when he apparently tried to get away from the officer guarding him. He fell and hit his head."

"Is he…"

"He died. Hemorrhaged. Nothing they could do."

She stared at Tommy for a moment before he pulled her into his arms and held her. Fitz was gone. She hated the relief she felt and reminded herself that she'd been pushed to the point that she'd wanted to kill him and might have if Tommy hadn't shown up when he did.

Fitz had been misguided and power hungry, but it seemed wrong to be so thankful that a childhood acquaintance was gone. She told herself that maybe now he was finally at peace. Because otherwise, she'd known that he wasn't finished with her. He would have come after her again. Only the next time, she might not have been able to get away.

She shuddered and Tommy held her closer.

"You're all right now," he said. "We're all right." She nodded against his chest. "It's all rainbows and sunshine from here on out."

Bella laughed and looked up at him. "Rainbows and sunshine," she said and kissed him. As long as they were together, it definitely would be.

Tommy was surprised to find all three of his brothers waiting for him at the new office a few days later. "What's going on?" he asked, sensing trouble.

"It's official," James announced and held up Tommy's framed PI license. "I thought I'd let you put it on the wall." Some of the posters and photos of the cowboys in their family were now on the walls of the ground-floor office.

Tommy took the framed license and spotted the hook next to his brother's PI license. "You left a lot of room on that wall," he commented.

"For Davey's and Willie's PI licenses," James said, and his brothers laughed.

"Who said we were quitting the rodeo?" Willie said.

Davey was quiet. When Tommy had told him that Carla Richmond down at the bank had asked about him, he'd seen how his brother had brightened. "That all she said?" Tommy had suggested that maybe Davy should stop by the bank and see her sometime. Davy had said that maybe he would. He was smiling when he said it.

"Even if I gave up the circuit, I'm not becoming a private eye," Willie said, shaking his head. "It's too dangerous. I got shot at and thrown in jail for the night before James bailed me out and all I was doing was helping you steal a bride." They all laughed.

"I guess time will tell," James said and motioned to the front of the building. "Tommy, you should check out our new sign."

He stepped out the front door and looked up. Colt Brothers Investigations. He couldn't help the sudden bump of his heart or the lump that rose to his throat. He was doing this.

Smiling, he stepped back inside. James had pulled out the blackberry brandy and the paper cups. They lifted their cups and the room suddenly grew very quiet. Tommy knew what they all were thinking about even before James made the toast.

"To Dad." His voice broke. "We haven't forgotten." They all nodded.

"We will find out the truth," Tommy said, and they all drained their cups.

# Chapter Twenty-Six

Bella wanted to pinch herself. She couldn't believe she was standing in front of a full-length mirror again wearing a wedding dress. This one was of her own choosing though and so were the shoes on her feet and that smile on her face was real, she thought as she winked at her reflection.

She glanced over at the woman next to her. Lorelei was also wearing a wedding dress. They grinned at each other. It had been James's idea that they have a double wedding on the Fourth of July.

"I would love that," Lori had said. "This could be fun, unless you haven't completely gotten over your last wedding."

Bella had laughed. In the time that had gone by, she'd put Fitz and what had happened behind her. The FBI had cleared her father and he was rebuilding the business and doing better than even she had hoped.

"We could get married at the ranch," Bella had offered. "Maybe an outside wedding by the river."

She hadn't been anxious to have another one in the barn and she'd realized that the Colt men didn't care where they got married—as long as they did.

She smiled to herself now, remembering the day Tommy had saved her. "Marry me," he'd said as he'd dropped to one knee after Ian had left them in woods. "I love you and I should have done this a long time ago. Come on, Bella, it isn't like you aren't already dressed for it."

They'd both laughed. She'd taken his hands and pulled him to his feet. "Remember when we were really little and we would pretend to get married?"

"I didn't think you'd remember that," he'd said.

"I remember everything the two of us did growing up," she'd said, smiling. "You promised me an outdoor wedding by the river."

He'd laughed. "A promise is a promise."

"I will marry you this summer if you still want to get married. Who knows, you might decide being a PI isn't for you and go back to the rodeo. It was your first love," she'd teased.

"You're my true first love and always have been," he'd said. "I will marry you this summer by the river. In the meantime, can I put a ring on it?"

Bella had looked down at the huge diamond on her hand. She'd slipped it off without a second thought and hurled it into the pines. Tommy had shaken his head in surprise. "Some kids will be searching for treasure like we did at that age, and they'll find it in the dried pine needles," she'd said laughing. "Can you imagine it?" She'd seen that he could. "I just hope it brings them happiness."

He'd pulled her into his arms for another kiss. Then he'd opened the small velvet box he'd taken from his pocket. She hadn't needed him to get on one knee again. He'd taken the small diamond ring from the box, and she'd held out her hand. It had fit perfectly. She'd smiled down at it on her hand and then up at Tommy. "It's exactly what I wanted."

"Ready?" Whitney asked from the doorway, bringing her out of her reverie. It would be a small wedding, just family and a few friends. There would be a campfire afterward. There would be beer and hot dogs over the fire, Colt family style even though Roberto had offered to cater their weddings.

She and Tommy would be moving into the ranch after they were married and she hoped Roberto would stay on as she rehired staff both for her business and the ranch.

"I've never been more ready," Bella said now.

Whitney got tears in her eyes. "I'm going to cry. After everything you've been through to finally find the man of your dreams?" She wiped her eyes and handed Bella her bouquet. This time it was daisies, reminding her of spring and new beginnings.

Tommy and James were waiting for them at the river along with the pastor who would be performing the ceremonies. Both men were dressed in Western attire, including their best boots and Stetsons.

"Colt men," Lori whispered. "Aren't they handsome."

"Especially Willie," Whitney said, making them both laugh.

But Bella had to admit, seeing the four brothers together like this, it took her breath away.

She looked at Tommy. He had a huge smile on his face that made her laugh. She knew that they'd been heading toward this moment since they first met all those years ago. She was marrying her best friend, her lover, her future. She couldn't wait to become his wife and join his family.

"We are going to make some adorable children," she said as she and Lori walked toward the altar they'd built by the river and Tommy waiting for her.

Lori giggled. "We've already started," she whispered.

Bella grinned over at her. "Congratulations. I suspect we won't be far behind," she said as she turned to meet Tommy's gaze. She was finally coming home to the one place she'd always belonged with the cowboy who'd stolen her heart at the age of four.

\* \* \* \* \*

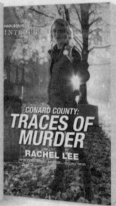

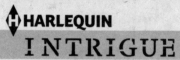
### #2079 SHERIFF IN THE SADDLE
*The Law in Lubbock County* • by Delores Fossen

The town wants her to arrest her former boyfriend, bad boy Cullen Brodie, for a murder on his ranch—but Sheriff Leigh Mercer has no evidence and refuses. The search for the killer draws them passionately close again...and into relentless danger. Not only could Leigh lose her job for not collaring Brodie...but they could both lose their lives.

### #2080 ALPHA TRACKER
*K-9s on Patrol* • by Cindi Myers

After lawman Dillon Diaz spent one incredible weekend with the mysterious Roslyn Kern, he's shocked to encounter her months later when he's assigned to rescue an injured hiker in the mountains. Now, battling a fiery blaze and an escaped fugitive, it's up to Dillon and his K-9, Bentley, to protect long-lost Rosie—and Dillon's unborn child.

### #2081 EYEWITNESS MAN AND WIFE
*A Ree and Quint Novel* • by Barb Han

Relentless ATF agent Quint Casey won't let his best lead die with a murdered perp. He and his undercover wife, Agent Ree Sheppard, must secretly home in on a powerful weapons kingpin. But their undeniable attraction is breaking too many rules for them to play this mission safe—or guarantee their survival...

### #2082 CLOSING IN ON THE COWBOY
*Kings of Coyote Creek* • by Carla Cassidy

Rancher Johnny King thought he'd moved on since Chelsea Black broke their engagement and shattered his heart. But with his emotions still raw following his father's murder, Chelsea's return to town and vulnerability touches Johnny's heart. And when a mysterious stalker threatens Chelsea's life, protecting her means risking his heart again for the woman who abandoned him.

### #2083 RETRACING THE INVESTIGATION
*The Saving Kelby Creek Series* • by Tyler Anne Snell

When Sheriff Jones Murphy rescues his daughter and her teacher, the widower is surprised to encounter Cassandra West again—and there's no mistaking she's pregnant. Now someone wants her dead for unleashing a secret that stunned their town. And though his heart is closed, Jones's sense of duty isn't letting anyone hurt what is his.

### #2084 CANYON CRIME SCENE
*The Lost Girls* • by Carol Ericson

Cade Larson needs LAPD fingerprint expert Lori Del Valle's help tracking down his troubled sister. And when fingerprints link Cade's sister to another missing woman—and a potentially nefarious treatment center—Lori volunteers to go undercover. Will their dangerous plan bring a predator to justice or tragically end their reunion?

"CHELSEA, WHAT'S GOING ON?" Johnny clutched his cell
phone to his ear and at the same time he sat up and turned
on the lamp on his nightstand.

"That man…that man is here. He tried to b-break in."
The words came amid sobs. "He…he was at my back
d-door and breaking the gl-glass to get in."

"Hang up and call Lane," he instructed as he got out
of bed.

"I…already called, but n-nobody is here yet."

Johnny could hear the abject terror in her voice, and an
icy fear shot through him. "Where are you now?"

"I'm in the kitchen."

"Get to the bathroom and lock yourself in. Do you hear me? Lock yourself in the bathroom, and I'll be there as quickly as I can," he instructed.

"Please hurry. I don't know where he is now, and I'm so scared."

"Just get to the bathroom. Lock the door and don't open it for anyone but me or the police." He hung up and quickly dressed. He then strapped on his gun and left his cabin. Any residual sleepiness he might have felt was instantly gone, replaced by a sharp edge of tension that tightened his chest.

*Don't miss*
Closing in on the Cowboy *by Carla Cassidy,*
*available July 2022 wherever*
*Harlequin Intrigue books and ebooks are sold.*

Harlequin.com

# HARLEQUIN

*Heartfelt or thrilling, passionate or uplifting—Harlequin is more than just happily-ever-after.*

With twelve different series to choose from and new books available every month, you are sure to find stories that will move you, uplift you, inspire and delight you.

HNEWS2021